Advance Praise for *Ch*

"Michelle Blair Wilker's work is a welcomed joy. Her unique diversity of storytelling coupled with her colorful prose makes the characters leap off the page. I highly recommend."

—Debbie Allen, Producer/Director

"In literature, as in music or even life, everything often comes down to discovering your own voice. Michelle Blair Wilker has found her voice as a writer—one that is smart, subtle, and sharp. So now it's our turn to discover her."

—David Wild, Writer & Author, Contributing Editor to *Rolling Stone*, Emmy-Nominated Television Writer

"Michelle Blair Wilker's writing has a lyrical quality to it, and she has a unique ability to impart both a sense of desperation and hints of hope in the same passage. She so succinctly conveys both setting and mood, that there's no need for wasted words."

—Kristen Hansen Brakeman, Author of *Is That the Shirt You're Wearing?*

"Michelle Blair Wilker writes about slices of life with unexpected turns, and though the characters are unique in their own ways, I find myself relating to them. I always look forward to her next story; she makes me laugh and she makes me think."

—Barry Jay, Writer of *The Chosen* and *Patient Seven*

"Michelle Blair Wilker writes with wit, passion, and insight. She has clearly observed life across her years and deftly translated it to the page."

—Brent Monahan, Author of *The Jekyl Island Club* series, *The Book of Common Dread*, and *An American Haunting*

chain linked

STORIES

Post Hill
PRESS

MICHELLE BLAIR WILKER

A POST HILL PRESS BOOK
ISBN: 978-1-68261-589-8
ISBN (eBook): 978-1-68261-590-4

Chain Linked:
Stories
© 2018 by Michelle Blair Wilker
All Rights Reserved
Cover art by Suppasak Viboonlarp

Post Hill Press
New York · Nashville
posthillpress.com

Published in the United States of America

For Zelda
With all my love
MBW

Special Thanks

Lawrence J. Wilker
and
Lou Reda

CONTENTS

BACKBURNER

◇◇◇◇◇◇◇◇◇◇◇◇◇◇◇◇◇◇◇◇◇◇◇◇◇◇◇◇◇◇◇◇◇◇◇◇

My friend Michael has a theory. Guys always have several burners going at once. Sometimes you're on high heat up front, and sometimes they move you to the back to simmer and bubble up slowly. They never focus on just one dish, cooking eggs, bacon, and spaghetti sauce at the same time. Occasionally, they stir and test the temperature, but mostly they're saving you for later. For when the fry pan up front gets crusty and cools down.

I'm definitely on the backburner. I can feel it. I got shifted up front for a split second. It gave me enough incentive to stay engaged, but it was like the flash of a summer firefly and now I'm on low behind the large soup tureen. Besides, who wants soup on a hot summer day? It's just an appetizer before the main course.

I try to sip my Mudslide, but the consistency is so dense that it cakes up the straw. I remove it and take a gulp of the creamy tannish liquid. Chocolate streaks line the glass, and it's chilly and lumpy as it travels down my throat. Mandy convinced me to come to Liars. I wanted to stay home, swing on the hammock, and feel sorry for myself. But here I am listening to her drunk as hell singing Sheryl Crow.

"Tip your fucking bartender," she chimes in after she screeches out a lyric. You would think it was a line in the song, because she yells it out every other minute.

I have been reduced to Friday-night karaoke at a dive bar in Montauk with the legendary local lesbian. We met Mandy last summer at Liars, where she insisted that we had hung out the previous year. We hadn't. But she was just nuts enough that we went along. She told me I had great cheekbones and that Harry had a fantastic sense of fashion. She wanted to discuss the Israeli–Palestinian conflict.

"Do you follow it?" she asked.

"Yes," Harry replied.

"Bullshit. Hey, you're pretty handsome. High five."

She smacked his hand, did a shot of bourbon, and went up for more Sheryl Crow.

"Tip your fucking bartender!"

It was like her anthem. The bar smelled of sea salt and beer, and the dark wood was scratched up and sticky. There were wall-to-wall people. The summer season had just begun, and all the Upper East Side douchebags had begun to arrive. Well, they don't usually come to Liars, but still it was quite crowded. Montauk makes me miss the East Coast. It's like the real world with genuine live people. Not shiny, blonde, tan humans with bright white teeth. There's grit, fisherman, loud Brooklyn accents, and beer bellies. You know where you stand. It's not like swimming in a murky sea of unknown intention and phony sentiment.

It's nice to sit in the real world, even if it's only for a few days. I can smell the rain too. Everything is fresh and green and I'm not thinking about my backburner status. I'm calm, I'm comfy, I'm present.

"Rach, c'mon. Let's do some Go-Go's. If I hear Mandy squeal out one more Sheryl Crow, I'm literally going to lose it."

Elisa is facing away from the bar staring at Mandy and attempting to drink her Mudslide. She's guzzling it down in thick chunks like it's ice cream. Mandy moves her hips back and forth and jumps up and down as she screams into the microphone. Her short, blonde hair bounces, and her acid-washed jean jacket looks a tad yellowish underneath the dim lights.

"I mean she's not in tune and making up half the lyrics."

Elisa was right, but Mandy was having a blast. You could see it in the way she danced, and frankly she didn't give a shit what anyone thought. She closed her eyes and smiled. The expression on her face said it all.

I visit Montauk every summer to see my old college roommate, Elisa, and her boyfriend, Harry. They live in Brooklyn but come to Montauk on weekends to escape the sweaty city and stench of rotten hot garbage. It's different out here. It makes you forget. It's serene and smells sweet. It reminds me of the Cape. All the cedar shake houses and lilac bushes, lobster rolls, clambakes, and families peddling along on bicycles. It's quaint and Norman Rockwellish. It's certainly not Los Angeles. An ocean of traffic jams, smog, and Botoxed flakes. The sun always shines like it's Groundhog Day. Nothing changes. Montauk makes me feel whole.

"I found 'We Got the Beat,'" Elisa says. "I signed us up. There are a million people in front, but who cares?" She slams her glass on the bar. It skims the surface and knocks over a saltshaker. Tiny granules sprinkle across the jagged wood like delicate snowflakes.

"Cool," I nod. Thankfully, we'll never sing. The queue is too long and if I know Elisa and Harry, they will get sick of waiting and want to go to 7-Eleven for late-night pizza and hot wings. Mudslides always give her the munchies.

I click my phone. No messages. It's been a week. I don't know why I care. It's not like this is the first time I've been shifted to the backburner. I got sucked in with sweet words, promises, and three months of daily messages. We were going to surf Lower Trestles and eat fish tacos, go to a Kings of Leon show at the Bowl, and wine taste in Santa Barbara. I wanted to believe it because what was the point? Why say it if you don't mean it? Meanwhile, he likes my vacation photos on Instagram. See "backburner."

Finally, we get a break from Sheryl. A tiny preppy redhead starts rapidly rhyming Kris Kross's "Jump." She's actually pretty good. She knows every word by heart and doesn't even glance at the monitor. The words zoom by so fast, I can't even read them. The Liars crowd cheers and claps noisily. The French couple next to me starts to hug each other and do some weird dance where they are tangled and hopping. It looks like a potato sack race. Good thing she fixed her shoe with duct tape five minutes ago. She propped her foot on the bar and wrapped six large pieces around the tip of her sneaker.

"It fixes anything." She lobbed the roll back to the bartender. "*Merci.*"

Mandy stands to the side bobbing her head, waiting patiently for her next opportunity. The little redhead's rendition is quite catchy, and I tap my sandal against the base of the stool. How does she even know the words? It looks like she isn't old enough to have been born when the song was top of the charts. Besides, those Kris Kross kids' rhyming was pretty complex and dope.

"Rach, stop checking your phone. Who cares about that guy? Not even worth a second thought."

"I wasn't checking." But she knows me. I dot my pinkie into several salt snowflakes, cleaning up some of the scattered flecks.

She's right, but the worst feeling in the world is to be ignored, disposed of, replaced. I feel worthless. Hollow like a rotting tree stump. Like something's wrong. Why didn't I get picked? I know it's not me, but there is that little voice deep down. That nagging nasty alter ego. The "glass half empty" me. The one that says *yup, it is you.* I'm not sad, I'm not heartbroken, but it stings a bit. Almost like a pesky mosquito bite.

"Hey there, hot stuff." Mandy is now pressed up against the bar and has her arm draped around my shoulder. Her face is two inches from mine, and I can smell a combination of smoke and cream on her breath.

"Check out the cheekbones on this fox." Mandy points above my head. "Mudslide for Mandy." And she bangs a twenty onto the bar.

Elisa has moved on from Mudslides to Coronas and is now sitting on Harry's lap in the corner. Her legs dangle and don't quite reach the floor. She's pretty drunk and flips her dark hair and giggles. Harry squeezes the back of my neck, shrugs, and then continues to watch the hockey game. He looks pretty worn out after spending all day laying Sheetrock in the laundry room. He's still got smatterings of white dust on the cuffs of his jeans.

Elisa and Harry take care of me and treat me like family. We don't talk all the time or see each other more than once or twice a year, but when we reunite it's like we were never apart. We don't skip a beat.

"Mands, tell Rachel to forget this West Coast asshole and his Real Housewife girlfriend."

"Forget 'im. You got me. Besides, who has cheekbones like you? Who could pass that up? What an idiot. I'll fix you up with a real man. What about that hunk in the lobster shorts?"

Mandy nods in the direction of the dock, where a tall guy with salt-and-pepper hair is chatting with friends. The boys are deeply sunburned under their eyes and wear various pastel shorts with scattered random objects. Crabs, tennis rackets, whales, and strawberries. Ray-Ban pilot glasses top their heads like shiny golden crowns.

"Thanks, but no thanks, Mands." The last thing I needed was Sheryl Crow's biggest fan to be my wingman.

"Suit yourself. But I got game."

Elisa and I glance at each other and try not to laugh. I take a large gulp of my Mudslide. I mean, Mandy is the best. You couldn't make it up if you tried.

"Thanks, lady. You sure do." I clap her on the back. Her jacket feels a bit damp. She flashes me the "hang ten" sign before heading up front to bully someone into letting her do more Sheryl.

I think I've come to terms with my backburner status. Maybe it just wasn't meant to be? Maybe I'm one of those people who is destined to be alone? To be the rainy-day option when it doesn't work out with the Playboy bunny or cheerleader. Fuck that. I'm not waiting around for when he comes to the realization that the shiny new object is insane. I'm good with it, yeah. Montauk has fixed me. Reminded me of who I am. It tugged at me deep down and said, "Hey, you're an East Coast girl at heart. Embrace it. You're real, you've got spunk, you've got me. Remember my pinky-orange sunsets; lumpy, steep sand dunes; and pebbled rocky shores. My decadent ice cream–filled summer and daily Ditch Plains surf sessions."

I glance at the front and see Mandy trying to convince the little redhead to do a duet. She's selling her everything she's got. She's making loud gestures and flashing her best "Mandy smile." The bar is loud, but through the muffled chatting and piercing Journey song I can hear a foghorn in the distance. The moon is a tiny golden sliver, and the sky is clear enough to see some twinkling stars. It's almost time to drive Harry and Elisa home. I can tell she's close to craving those hot wings.

My phone buzzes and slides across the salty surface.

HEY GIRL! HOW ARE YOU?!?! ;)

I study the energetic text and silly emoticon and without hesitation press Delete. I take a deep breath, my shoulders relax, and that thick, twisted tummy knot loosens. I let out a chuckle.

"Hey, can I buy you a cocktail?" Lobster Shorts is standing next to me and grinning. He's pretty cute, even with his Ray-Ban crown at 10 p.m. His eyes have tiny creases underneath, and his pink shirt is buttoned all lopsided.

"Sure."

Mandy's back to Sheryl again. This time she's playing a little air guitar and has removed the acid-washed jean jacket. She stops, points at me, and winks before going back to shouting into the microphone. You would think she was playing Madison Square Garden.

"Cheers," Lobster Shorts says.

"Tip your fucking bartender!"

LAST GLIMPSE OF FRED

◇◇◇◇◇◇◇◇◇◇◇◇◇◇◇◇◇◇◇◇◇◇◇◇◇◇◇◇◇◇◇◇◇◇◇◇

Frederico Villa de Bastardo waited patiently outside La Oficina de Emigración, clutching his rumpled papers. The bottlenecked queue was at least sixty people deep. Fred tilted his head northbound and counted all the *cabezas*, some topped with straw cowboy hats, others crowned with pastel parasols.

"*¿Dios mío, que es esto?*" He fanned the papers just below his chin, puffing out a tiny breeze. It stunk of burnt plantains and sweat.

It was a blistering and humid day in Havana and it was only 9 a.m. The sun had just begun to eke out its scorching fury, pelting an unbearable wrath on the back of Fred's shoulders. He shrugged, attempting to knock it from his sizzling flesh, and reshuffled the letter of invitation and *permiso* from work. He patted his pants pocket for cash for the visa and exit permit. It had taken nine months to save up all his tips as a *guía turístico*. Fred studied at *la Universidad Nacional* to become a lawyer, but took a job with *Transtur Havana*. It was three times the salary, so he did not return for the third year. A tour guide was a good living in Cuba.

"*Papi*, where do you think you are you going?" asked the tiny *mujer*.

She tugged at his *guayabera* and indicated the papers he was fanning. Her short gray hair was soaked from the heat and glistened when just the right amount of sun speckled at its apex.

"Roma!"

"Fat chance of that." She spun, waddling a few steps and dragging her sandals along the asphalt.

Fred clicked his tongue and shook his head. What did she know? Crazy old lady should mind her own business anyway.

"Don't listen to her. This is her fifth time trying to get to Miami to see her grandchildren," said the *vaquero detrás*.

He towered a good three inches above Fred, and his sombrero added a bumpy wave to the sea of straw. A thin leather band encircled it as a feather jutted up. If Fred squinted, the hats blended together into a spectacular golden haze.

"*Gracias, señor.*" Fred removed his baseball cap and bowed.

"*El comandante* doesn't grant visitation to *madres* of defectors."

He almost shouted it, which was most certainly intended for the tiny *mujer* to hear, but she ignored him and hobbled onward.

Fred smiled. Three hours had passed since he had joined the queue, and there were still fifteen people ahead. At least now he could glimpse the entrance with the large poster of Fidel and Raul saluting in their official military garb.

La Revolución Pujante y VICTORIOSA Sigue Adelante—The Powerful and Victorious Revolution Continues.

"Sort of," Fred muttered as he read the text over and over to pass the time. He wasn't much for propaganda with it shoved down your throat every two meters. "Enough Fidel, we get it. It's been fifty years."

Underneath the poster, Fred spotted paint peels. Some had remnant chips dangling by microscopic threads. The building was filthy with flaxen water marks and soiled blemishes. He was surprised that it was still standing. An edifice crumbled practically every day in Havana. It would plummet in a crescendo like a concrete waterfall and kick up plumes of dust and sharp pebbles in its wake. There was no mistaking the noise as it crashed with a reverberating thud. But Fred was used to it. Everyone in Havana was.

"*¿Roma? No te creo,*" said the *vaquero*. "Why?"

"*Mi amigo* Mario Biscotti lives there, and I want to tour the Vatican and eat some good pizza."

"*Coño, que suerte!*"

"What about you?"

"Miami, like the rest of these poor bastards. My great-aunt has lived there since before *la revolución.*"

"Wow. Not many of those left."

"*Asi mismo, es verdad.*"

"Good luck, *mi amigo.*"

"*Gracias.*"

Fred made it inside just shy of the vestibule. The clerks were inspecting documents and stamping them with a snap and a whistle. It was just a matter of time before his turn would arrive. The butterflies skittered from one end of his tummy to the other like a swarm of daddy longlegs. He had waited so patiently and saved for so long. It's not like he was a doctor or professor. His job was of no consequence to *el gobierno.*

Mario had sent him countless letters and photos of the places they would visit. The Trevi Fountain, Colosseum, and Roman Forum, all blindingly ornate, some encased in pearly marble. Roman architecture was so masterful and ancient, and yet it did not crumble the way it did in Havana, a city littered with rubble and dotted with vacant casino high-rises that haunted the Malecón with their loneliness. It was mortifying.

"*Compañero.*"

The clerk beckoned, flailing his hands skyward. *Gracias a Dios.*

"*Buenos días.*" Fred arrayed his papers on the counter and shuffled them into a neat pile. The clerk was a lanky fellow with his head plopped on top like a child's lollipop. A nametag identified him as Pedro. He pushed his spectacles up the bridge of his nose and didn't say "good morning." He then went to examining the documents. Fred tapped his index finger just outside the counter and peeked next door. The tiny *mujer* had tears streaming down her face. She gripped a wrinkly paper sphere. "*Por favor,*" she bawled. *El hombre* to his left arranged family photos into a rainbow, clutching his straw hat tight.

"My beautiful grandchildren. They miss me," he said.

Fred was mesmerized by all the pleas and continued to tap. Pedro stared, so Fred clasped his hands behind his back. Was he supposed to make conversation or just be quiet? A friendly demeanor was always best. Abuela said that there was no excuse for a lack of manners.

"It's a beautiful day today, although it's *hace mucho calor.*" Fred let out a toothy grin, but Pedro just continued to flip each page with a rustling whip.

What a self-important ass. These civil servants had sticks shoved so far up their backsides that they thought they were Fidel themselves. Rendering judgments and enforcing policies they knew nothing about, but Fred continued to smile.

The room was serene despite how crowded it was. People were on top of each other like icing slathered all over a *tres leches.* Hats flapped to circulate oxygen, and a hushed murmur clung and then trickled down from the crown moldings in bits and drabs. Fred's curls inflated into a stout mushroom.

"*Compañero Bastardo*, your host in Roma is a taxicab driver?"

"*Sí, señor.*"

"Did you bring the fee?"

"*Sí.*"

Fred pulled out the cash and counted it, laying out one bill at a time. Pedro seized it and banged it like it was a deck of playing cards.

"Wait here."

The *vaquero* signaled the thumbs-up.

Pedro's silhouette reflected in the large windowpane; he was gesturing with his pencil. Fred tried to inch closer, but as his head gained measure, the image dissipated into a blur. Oh well, he would find out soon enough.

"*Compañero Bastardo*, thank you for your patience."

"*Por supuesto.*"

"I'm sorry to say, but *el jefe* has determined that a taxi driver from Roma cannot afford to sponsor you. You can reapply in six months and return with the proper documentation and requisite fees."

He imprinted *NEGADO* on the application. The crimson ink trickled out in bloody streaks.

"Next."

"*Por favor, señor*. Please reconsider. Mario makes quite a good living in Roma. I promise he can afford it."

Pedro shoved the wounded documents under the plexi. The imprint smudged into a gory Rorschach.

"Next."

Fred gripped his denial. Woozy and heated, he backed away, trying to skate one foot behind the other. His left shoe was affixed to the sticky linoleum, and he stumbled. Cheap bastards couldn't even manage to clean the floor. He clenched his fists, curling them into sticky pink mounds. He needed to leave before he punched Pedro in *la boca*. Then he would never make it to Roma. Like, ever.

It was still hot outside, and sweat trickled off his forehead like a leaky faucet.

"Watch it, asshole," shouted a taxi driver in a maroon Lada.

He honked. Fred popped up his middle finger; he was in no mood. Brightly colored Buicks and Chevrolets paraded past. They hauled tourists snapping photos. *Turistas* ate that vintage shit up, especially the Yankees from the *Estados Unidos*. Little did they know they were spackled together from Russian spare parts and that two blocks away, tarnished cadavers rested in broken-down heaps abandoned in alleyways. Fred kicked the curb and scrunched up his rejection.

He found himself down by the *Malecón*. Oblivious sweethearts held hands and shared ice cream, basking in their delusional bubble. Their feet dangled just a few inches off the ground. It smelled of salt and rotten *pescado*. He had spent close to six hours trying to get that visa and turned down a group from the U.S., the biggest tippers by far. It would take him another nine months to save up again. What a fucking racket.

Abuela would be so disappointed. He planned to bring her back a rosary from the Vatican. Surfers on ramshackle boards floated, awaiting that epic wave, but the heat and lack of wind killed the current. Fred could see that the black flags had been taken down from the U.S. embassy since George W. Bush left office. That Obama fellow didn't seem too bad. Hell, anyone was better than Jorge.

He rested against the wall, gravel tickling his spine. God, he hated Fidel. His ears swelled, and blood percolated just below the surface. He wasn't a whiny traitor; he just wanted a decent piece of pizza. Fred lived quite well here. Abuela owned their home, and Mario had given him an iPhone. He was lucky. He witnessed the squalor as he walked to work every day. Tiny Mía who clutched her colorful caged door. Barefoot with dirt smudges lining her chubby cheeks, dressed in only white cotton underwear and a ripped T-shirt.

"*Hola, hola, hola!*" she sang until he answered back.

Her toddler image was branded into his psyche. He looked forward to and yet dreaded this daily visit. When was a revolution no longer a revolution and just a shitty way of life?

It was almost time for supper, and Abuela was waiting. He took one last glance down the line of the *Malecón*. Fishermen cast their lines with lengthy swoops, and baby waves lapped up the wall. Ah, fuck it, Cuba.

–✸–

"*Mi vida.* Tell me everything. When do you leave?"

Abuela was stirring beans from a medium-sized pot. Smoke wafted from its base. She grinned and clutched a large wooden spoon. Her hair was twisted into a neat snowy bun, and her apron had grease marks peppering its hem.

"*Negado.*"

"*Oye, chico,* but you are such a great patriot!"

"The communists can eat my shit."

"Frederico!"

"Sorry, Abuela. It's just not right."

Fred sank at the kitchen table and glared at the scratched-up wood. It was mahogany with ornate floral engravings on each leg. Abuela inherited it from her mother, who had been quite the socialite in the '50s. He had seen pictures of her in slinky evening gowns, dripping in jewels, finger waves adorning her curls as she made her way to The Tropicana.

"Frederico, are you listening to me?"

Abuela tapped him on the shoulder with her spoon. He could smell the lard starting to saturate. No, he wasn't, but he nodded anyway. He would get approved soon enough. Fidel was testing him. *El Comandante* knew how to weed out the weak and unworthy. Only the strong prevailed, so he must not give up. After forty years, the propaganda permeated deep.

"You are a nice young man, loyal. Not like Carlos De La Cruz. You deserve this."

"Abuela, that was ten years ago. He was only nineteen."

Carlos lived in their *barrio* and they had been friends as *niños*, although Abuela never liked him. He disfigured *gobierno* propaganda and wrote nasty poetry about *la revolución*. He spent eight months concocting a makeshift boat out of an old porcelain bathtub and a lawn mower engine. He puttered that contraption all the way to Miami in the dead of night, and Fred hadn't seen him since. Abuela never forgot his treachery. She could barely muster a polite wave to his mother but always tried. A lady never forgot her manners.

"Don't you worry, Mijo."

She scrunched up a handful of curls, patted him on the back, and clanked the spoon against the pan.

–❈–

It had barely cooled down even though it was close to midnight; the moon cast a spotlight across the center of his bed. Fred sweated all over his sheets and drifted in and out. Visions of Che and Fidel cackled as they slurped up long spaghetti noodles. Marinara sauce dripped and splashed over the red-checked tablecloth like a violent bloodbath. They toasted clinking glasses of Chianti and swayed to the light tinkling of an accordion. Fred shot up. This was ridiculous. He had to get to Roma, no matter what.

He was exhausted by the time he got up. The sun rose with its pinky glow, and roosters let out their cock-a-doodle-doos. *La vecina* De La Cruz walked her puppy down *la calle*. The little guy's fur was freckled with coffee-colored specks. He stopped every few meters to sniff random blades of grass, focusing on the weeds surrounding Fred's mailbox.

"*Buenos días.*"

"*Hola, como estas*, Frederico?"

He turned to see if Abuela was still inside. She didn't usually get up this early, but you never knew with her.

"How is Carlos?"

"*Bien.* I got a letter from him last week. I miss him, but you know, he was going *loco* here. It's for the best."

"*Sí, entiendo.* I think of him often and wonder about that crazy boat he built."

"You and me both. He went to the library and read a million books on mechanics and engineering. *Que genio.*"

"*Es verdad.* Well, I'm off." He tipped his cap, releasing those crazy curls.

"*Adios.* Say hello to your grandmother."

Fred nodded and strapped on his backpack. He waved. How could Carlos fabricate a boat out of junkyard scraps by just reading at the library? He must have had help. Fred didn't have a mind for physics, and even if he did it's not like he could pilot a vessel all the way to Italy. Abuela would never forgive him; it was just the two of them since Mamá had passed on. What was he thinking?

This week Fred's group was from the U.S. He usually worked with Italian tourists. That's how he met Mario. The Yankees were lively and full of questions.

"Does the government own the golf course? The Hotel Nacional?"

"Remember when I said there are no stupid questions?" Fred rolled his eyes.

Sometimes it was difficult to have patience for their ignorance, but they amused him with their opulence and brash nature. They were kind and offered to sponsor him to the U.S., but he had no interest. It was Roma or *nada*.

Havana's constant heat wave had roasted the island into a nice, slow pace. The *Malecón* was crowded with folks splashing off the humidity, and La *Biblioteca Nacional* was nearly empty even though it was Saturday. It was much cooler inside, so Fred wasn't sure why they didn't all march down from the *Malecón* and pretend to read, like the rest of the patrons. He had searched through the card catalogs for two hours to find books on boat engineering and Italian architecture. He needed to understand how Carlos had done it, but none of it made any sense. It was like trying to read Chinese when you didn't know the characters.

He slammed an *Introducción a la Ingeniería Naval* shut and flipped through the architecture one. What was he doing here? He just wanted to be a tourist on vacation. The colors of the Sistine Chapel were vibrant. Their beauty made his blood crackle. He had seen the images a million times but never got weary of them. He packed up the books and returned them to the librarian up front. She was on her tippy-toes reshelving. She slid a book at a time in, plugging up the gaps like a gigantic puzzle. Fred loved *la biblioteca*, especially as a *niño*; it was peaceful, and the musty smell was intoxicating. He could escape to anywhere or be anyone.

He took his work route home. An *hola* from Mía would be nice right now. A cute pout and a tiny giggle. The cobblestones were shattered and poked straight up. He had to skip over a few. Rusted automobiles dotted the path, frozen in time and left for dead bygone-era grandeur. Two stray *perros* trailed. One was missing a leg but hobbled; she yelped a little. The street looked a bit odd, spacious and vacant. An old garnet Pontiac rested on the curb with its front tires deflated and the PONT missing. Only the IAC remained, and the street sign above read Calle San Ignacio. Yes, this was right. Fred shrugged. He was tired and needed a good nap. Fidel and Che still haunted him nightly with their Italian adventuring.

He rounded the corner and halted. Exposed pewter beams survived above a tower of bulky rubble. His stomach plummeted to his knees. He spun until the landscape melded into a rainbow of chaos.

"Mía, Mía!"

He sprinted back and forth, stopping to lift up chunks of wreckage. Bits of filthy laundry and shattered furniture were buried, as lilac petals and blades of grass fought their way to the surface.

"Mía, Mía!"

Fred gasped and jumped on top of the Pontiac to get a better view.

"*Mía!*"

It was silent; a tumbleweed could have blown past.

He leapt off.

"*Jesús, por favor.*"

Fred's voice echoed. He stopped and panted.

"*Hola, hola, hola.*"

He cupped a hand over his ear like he was eavesdropping on a seashell.

"*Hola, hola, hola.*"

It was faint but high-pitched. He raced, following its melodic tune, footsteps pounding.

And there they were. Two streets over, walking barefoot and covered in filth. Sand kicked up as they strolled. Mía clutched her *mamá's* pinkie and skipped into a puddle. A bandage wrapped up her wrist mummy style.

"*Ay gracias. Dios mío. Que pasó?*" Fred asked Mía's *mamá*.

"The house collapsed two days ago. We are living with my *papá* and came back to collect some personal items. I know, it's a long shot, but…"

"Are you okay?"

"*Sí.*"

She gazed skyward as a tear escaped. She brushed it away, smudging the dirt stains further.

"*Hola, hola, hola.*"

Mía's hazel eyes were radiant. She hopped and grinned.

"*Hola*, my sweet."

Fred patted her knotted hair. Hopefully, she wouldn't remember this. She was so little and didn't know any different. He envied her innocence. To not know who Fidel was or understand what *la revolución* meant, to be able to enjoy a mud puddle and inhale sweet mariposas. To not comprehend that she no longer had a home.

Mía wrapped herself around his leg and hummed, "Fred, Fred." She never managed to squeeze out the "erico" portion.

"C'mon, Mía, leave Fred alone. We need to get back to *papá's* before it's dark."

"*Lo siento. Por favor*, let me know if you need anything."

"*Gracias.*"

She picked up Mía and propped her on her hip.

"*Adios*, Fred."

Mía raised her tiny hand and blew a filthy kiss.

"*Adios*, beautiful."

He watched until they were two specks dotting the horizon. He hesitated at what was once Mía's front door, and picked up a large chunk of debris and hurled it into the vacant lot, screaming at the top of his lungs.

–✦–

Nine months passed since he had last seen Mía and her *mamá*. Fred had never been on an airplane, and the daddy longlegs scratched at his belly with jittery delight. José Martí International Airport was crowded with tons of tourists and compatriots making their way to and from Miami.

"See, Mijo. I told you, it would work out in the end."

Abuela smirked. He hated that she was right. Well, only half right. He saved up again and waited, but Mario's brother, an employee of the Vatican, was his sponsor this time. *Estúpido* clerk couldn't argue with that profession.

"You are so strong, Mijo, and Fidel knew it. He is rewarding you."

"Abuela, I don't want to talk about *El Comandante*, okay?"

"Okay, Mijo."

She fiddled with his necktie and smoothed out his sport coat. He looked so grown-up and handsome. Tall with curls combed down into a neat bundle, skin tanned.

"Promise to send postcards and take lots of pictures." He nodded.

"*Te quiero mucho.*"

"*Te quiero*, Abuela."

Fred gathered up his duffel and tapped his jacket for the documentation and passport. He kissed Abuela on the cheek and shuffled into line. Passengers nudged and bumped, but it was okay. He was on his way to Italy. A propaganda poster hung from the wall just after the ticket agent: Hasta La Victoria Siempre—Ever Onward to Victory. He wasn't going to miss those.

Abuela dabbed her eyes with a tissue. She had lost track of him in the mob; they were clumped together in a colossal herd howling. She climbed on top of a bench and scanned the terminal. There he was. It was her last glimpse of Fred. The ticket agent was rifling through his papers and then returned them. Fred twirled and smiled. He walked towards the airplane with purpose and direction, shining with long strides. He then poked his head around the corner and gave a final wave before disappearing down the jetway.

MAC

◇◇◇◇◇◇◇◇◇◇◇◇◇◇◇◇◇◇◇◇◇◇◇◇◇◇◇◇◇◇◇◇◇◇

The empty classroom smelled of clay and papier-mâché. It was musty, thick, and cool. Mac breathed in the aroma. He wanted to imprint its essence into his brain. He took two shallow breaths, basking in the simplicity of it. It was funny how glue and dirt could make you smile. The lights were off, but through the large windowpanes he could see the sun creep its way lower and lower. It was a tiny sliver but sparkled and left a golden orange hue on the center table. He continued to straighten up, pushing in tiny wooden chairs and picking up wayward paintbrushes and pieces of charcoal. His hands were full of multi-colored speckles and chalk dust. They shook a little as he grabbed the last brush.

"Mac, you old coot," he said to himself as he dropped them in the sink. The water was a rainbow-garbled puddle.

He limped a little as he made his way. That bum-knee injury from Korea and the extra weight he'd gained over the last ten years made cleanup tricky. He was slow as honey on a hot summer day. Damn those oatmeal cookies. He just couldn't resist. Especially when they were baked just right. Not too chewy and not too crispy. Tessa would probably bring him another batch when she came down from the high school to take him to dinner.

He packed up his desk, placing the contents into a cardboard banker's box. He laid the calligraphy pens on top of his sketchpads and Princeton brushes. Most of the desk contained junk, loose papers, and pencil drawings, so he shuffled them into the wastebasket below. He opened the side closet and pulled out his worn leather satchel. There was a mirror on the interior, and he gazed at his reflection. His white hair dipped into a large swirl, and he pushed his thick black glasses up the bridge of his nose. God, he was fat. What did he expect? He was seventy years old, for Christ's sake. He took out his navy cable-knit cardigan and yanked down the picture of Oliver, his pug. He tossed them both on top of the satchel and slammed the closet door shut. It vibrated back and forth and didn't close, but he didn't care.

"Mr. MacDonald, how are you doing?"

Mac turned. Eleanor Zimmerman was waiting at the door. Her blonde hair was tied up in a neat French twist, and she wore a gray sweater draped over her shoulders. She was clutching a rectangular box.

"Hello, Eleanor. I'm managing just fine. Thank you very much."

What the hell did she want? He wasn't in the mood for the PTA. He groaned and attempted a weak smile. "Do you need something? I'll leave the keys on the counter by the sink on my way out." He packed up the last remaining items on the desk.

"Oh, no. Don't worry about that. I brought you a little gift from the PTA. Boy, we are going to miss you!" She took a few tentative steps into the classroom and let out a nervous chuckle. It was high-pitched like a hyena, and he could see that she had lipstick stains on her teeth. She outstretched her toothpick arms and offered him the box.

Mac blushed. He felt a bit guilty for being crabby, but not that guilty. He was old and tired, and this retirement business was quite draining.

"Thanks, Eleanor. You guys shouldn't have." He took the box and bowed his head.

"Open it!" She was now biting on her bottom lip and rocking back and forth on her heels.

"Okay."

Mac shuffled over to the counter and plopped the box down. He pried it open with the X-acto knife he carried in the left breast pocket of his baby blue smock. He sliced it along each taped side, creating a crooked line. He pulled off layers of bubble wrap to see an eight-by-ten black-and-white photo on matte board. It was encased in a simple black frame. The photo was of him and some of his students from the 1960s. He was leaning over a sketchpad, and four boys were watching him as he drew. He was a lot thinner but still had the same swoop in his hair, thick glasses, and smock. The text underneath was in a flowery calligraphy. It read: Duncan P. MacDonald, Art Teacher Emeritus 1954–1991.

Mac ran his fingers over the glass. He saw his old-man reflection on top of his younger self. He took his glasses off and squinted to see if he could remember the names of any of the students, but he was too old and his memory was shot. This was back when the school had only boys. They were dropped off in wood-paneled station wagons at the main-hall turnaround. They had to wear a jacket and tie and shake the headmaster's hand every morning. Those were the good ole days when kids had manners and respect. Where had the time gone? What had he done with his life? Taught a bunch of rich prep school brats.

"Do you like it?" Eleanor was leaning over his shoulder. He could feel her warm breath on the back of his neck.

"I just love that photo. We are going to hang one up in the checkerboard lobby."

"It's great," Mac whispered. "Really, thank the PTA and the board." He touched his heart and closed his eyes.

"We are really going to miss you!" She patted him on the back like he was a kindergartener.

Who was that man in that photo? Did he still exist? And who was going to care when he was gone? He was just a dumb middle school art teacher.

"Mac!"

Tessa had a backpack fastened to both shoulders and was carrying a small polished blue tin. Her auburn curly hair was tied up in a loose ponytail.

"Hi, Tessa, we heard you are going to Yale next fall. Congrats!"

"Thanks, Mrs. Zimmerman!"

"Hey, kiddo!"

Mac pointed at Eleanor, making the cuckoo sign. Her back was to him. She turned and he quickly clasped his hands in front.

Tessa giggled.

"Well, Mr. MacDonald. Enjoy the photo. Thanks for everything you have done. I don't know what we will do without you."

"Thanks, Eleanor. I'm sure you guys will figure it out."

"Bye, Tessa. Drop us a line when you get to Connecticut." Eleanor re-adjusted the gray merino and glided out of the classroom, clicking her heels against the linoleum.

"Hey, a visit from the PTA! Now that's big!" Tessa strolled in and handed him the blue tin.

"This better not be what I think it is." He plucked the lid off and tugged at a layer of wax paper. It smelled of cinnamon and raisins.

"How am I going to marry a rich grandma if you keep making me fat? I will ration myself to one a day to make them last."

"You always say that."

Her blue eyes looked vivid and bright. Mac never had any kids of his own, but if he had a granddaughter, he would have imagined her to be just like Tessa.

"You still pulling that one?" Tessa pointed to the blackboard, where A CLOSED MOUTH CATCHES NO FLIES was written over and over in a neat curlicue script.

"The Cunningham kid kept mouthing off, so I gave him a project."

"I love that you never change. I feel awful for all the kids who don't get to have you."

"Oh, they won't even know the difference." He took a cookie out and crunched in. Perfection.

"Mac, don't eat one now. You will ruin your appetite."

She had her arms folded in front and shook her head, but she had a slight grin. She had such a pretty smile. Perfect, straight teeth. He waved her off and continued to chew. He brushed crumbs off his chin and placed the tin in the banker's box. Tessa sat down on a stool by the counter and began to spin.

"So, smarty-pants, Yale! You're going to forget about little old me when you go off to college with the big shots." Mac lowered himself onto the stool next to her. His knees creaked and his big belly rested on his thighs.

"I'll never forget you, Mac." She stopped spinning and leaned her elbow onto the counter. Her face was loaded with freckles.

"I don't wanna go to Yale. I'm going to be the dumbest one there. I bet they made a mistake and meant to accept another Tessa Clarke."

She glanced down and tapped her tennis shoe on the rim of the stool's base. She still had her backpack strapped on, hunched over like large sea turtle.

"Oh, Tessa. Don't say that. You are at the beginning of your journey. This will be a new challenge. You will do your best, as you always do. Give each new experience your best, but be happy with your success and happy in yourself. That's all you can do."

Mac shrugged and patted her forearm. Tessa nodded but was still looking down at her tennis shoes.

"Listen to me. I'm an old fart and I know better."

"Okay. Thanks, Mac. You're the best." Her eyes were a bit dewy but not a drop of liquid escaped. She sighed, managed a slight smile, and gave him a tiny punch on the shoulder.

What he wouldn't give to switch places with her. There was so much to look forward to, and here he was viewing life in the rearview mirror. This kid was going places. She was such a smart cookie and so sweet. There was nothing she couldn't accomplish. He was sure of it. He couldn't say the same about himself. He was at the end. It was too late to fix past mistakes. He felt like an old jalopy running out of steam. He would just putt-putt his way to whatever was left. Mac wasn't feeling sorry for himself; it was just a statement of facts. It was what it was.

"Mac, do you guys still make papier-mâché animals and paint copies of the *Mona Lisa*?"

"Yep. It's funny to see what the new kids come up with. One kid made a Mickey Mouse *Mona Lisa*."

"That's a good one. So, what's next for you? Are you going to travel and take exotic vacations? Drink piña coladas and lounge by the pool?"

What was he going to do? He had no family, no hobbies to speak of.

"Me and Oliver are going to hightail it down to South Beach and pick up some widows. We are going to take up shuffleboard and play bingo on Sunday nights."

"No really! What will you do?" She went back to her stool, spinning.

"Actually, I'm not quite sure." He was surprised that he had said it out loud.

"Well, you should definitely do something fun. That Miami scenario isn't half bad. Just think about all you can do. You have a new journey ahead of you too."

"Well, I don't know about that."

"I do. I expect a postcard from Miami and a picture of you and Oliver relaxing under a large rainbow umbrella." She glared at him.

He nodded thoughtfully and smiled, but just to make her feel better.

"Hey, we should probably head to dinner. I'm going to pull the car around." Tessa hopped off the stool and headed over to Mac's desk, where she grabbed the banker's box and clutched it low by her thighs.

"You coming?"

"Yeah, yeah. Give me a minute. I gotta grab a few things. I'll meet you out front."

Mac placed both hands on his knees as he made his way to standing. Those stools were not the easiest to disembark from. Tessa began to skip in the direction of the door, but when she reached the frame she whirled. The contents of the banker's box clinked together lightly.

"You were the best teacher I ever had." She flashed him her lovely smile and then continued on.

Mac stood alone in the middle of his classroom. He had a large lump at the base of his throat, and he felt a few unruly tears trickle down his wrinkled, plump cheek. The classroom was now dark, as the sun had set completely. Lights from the parking lot cast various shadows on the worktables and yet at the same time illuminated the paint supplies and kiln. He couldn't move an inch. He closed his eyes for a minute and began to take in a few substantial breaths. His lips were moist, and he could taste the salt from the teardrops on the tip of his tongue. He flicked his eyes open and limped his way over to the desk. He unbuttoned the baby blue smock and packed it in the tan satchel. He lugged the navy cardigan on and rolled up the sleeves to three-quarters. The dagger-and-thistle tattoo on his right forearm was now visible. He picked up the eight-by-ten photo of his younger self and stared at it for a minute before tossing the classroom keys on the counter. They slid across the smooth surface and made a loud spiraling clank as they traveled. He stood in the doorway to take one last glance around. Such a familiar sight, but also so foreign. He didn't belong here anymore. He took a final inhalation of the stale dirt and glue and shuffled his way outside the classroom. He faced the door and tugged on the brass knob to shut it with a tiny, insignificant click.

THAT DAY AT BERGDORF'S

◇◇◇◇◇◇◇◇◇◇◇◇◇◇◇◇◇◇◇◇◇◇◇◇◇◇◇◇◇◇◇◇◇◇◇◇◇◇

It was a dreary Saturday. The sidewalks were slick and washed clean from the drizzle. The smell of rotten garbage gave way to a fresh minty odor. My heels didn't have that familiar click. They squeaked when they made contact with the pavement. I just wanted to stare at the sparkly diamonds in the jewelry department. I ran my fingers along the shiny glass case; it felt cool as I dragged each digit along the smooth surface. Bergdorf's was always the perfect temperature. Warm, like dipping your toes into the water at the Miami seashore. The chandeliers oozed with elegance. Looking up, I got lost in their brilliance. The crystals melded, glistened, and hypnotized me. It was almost too much, and made me blink. And then I sorta saw his jumbled fat fingers in front of me.

He wasn't smiling, and I had to blink again to make sure it was really him. He was more robust than I remembered from last time, and his pinstripe necktie was askew, propping up his bowling ball cranium. I got kicked out of furs last week. I was walking from mink to mink petting them. I might have rubbed my cheek on one or two, but I don't think he saw me.

"Only serious customers, miss." He gestured his hefty paws towards the glass doors.

I used to work in handbags. My friend Trudy introduced me to Mrs. Friedlander, who ran ladies' accessories. Trudy worked in the glove department. We took the L from Lorimar station and changed to the N&R at 14th street. We had lunch together. Ma always made me bologna sandwiches with mustard and a side of fruit cup. She packed it in a brown paper sack. I loved being a working girl and taking the train into the city. Ma was so proud. She waved at me every morning from the stoop in her terry robe, but three months ago I got laid off. I didn't have the heart to tell her, so I still went into the city every day.

It was easy to spend hours at Bergdorf's trying on hats for church and watching the society ladies model cotillion gowns. Puffy white-cream confections and pink cotton candy mirages. At first, he would just glance, but then he trailed me as I made my way from department to department. He reeked of musty cigars and sweat and waddled like a penguin.

"May I help you, miss?"

"Back again, miss?"

"Please leave, miss."

He kicked me out five times last month. For no good reason, other than he thinks I'm trash. The hem on my coat was uneven, but I pressed it every night. I wore my Sunday best. I'm a good girl.

Now he grabbed my elbow and dragged me from the belt of my overcoat towards the foggy glass doors.

"I warned you last time."

My elbow throbbed and I jerked it away.

It was still raining, and I could feel trickles of moisture dot my face as he pinned me against the retailer's damp exterior.

"You are not welcome at Bergdorf's."

I looked at him but he couldn't see me. I shoved his bulky bicep and clocked his shins with the tip of my umbrella. I swung it like I was playing a round of golf. He doubled over and then slid onto the sidewalk like a beached whale.

"Miss..."

I sprinted without glancing back, clutching my umbrella tight. I popped it up when I got three blocks away, slowing to a jog. He didn't know me. I just wanted to be a working girl at Bergdorf's.

MANOLOS AND GAS FUMES

The Volvo was out of gas. I couldn't believe it. I can still hardly believe it. The red light dinged on the dashboard, exposing a tiny outline of a gas pump. It looked like a miniature neon sign. "C'mon down to Mobil," it warned. I hummed along to the radio. 98.7 was having a classic-rock weekend, and "Moondance" oozed out of the speakers. Earlier, the pinky-lemon sun sunk into the horizon, and it felt like one of those Indian summer nights when the air was still hot. Hot like a sauna. My window was open, and the balmy breeze blew my hair. Sometimes it blew it right into my mouth and I had to spit it out. I could taste the dry split ends. Time for a haircut.

And then the old gal sputtered, coughed, and halted. She was a rustic cadaver with headlights casting a shimmering glow over the valley. I was on Coldwater, and it was 1 a.m. This piece of shit has cost me a bloody fortune. Every time I took her to the dealer, he found a mechanical problem between 975 and 1500 dollars. I know. Never take it to the dealer, but I didn't know a good local mechanic.

"Lizzie, do you listen to *Car Talk?*" my pops asked me on the phone. "They might have some ideas. Those guys are terrific."

Like I was going to listen to a radio show that talked about cars. I'm not a dude. Anyway, I remembered that the car was not falling to shit; I was just an idiot. I ignored the red neon light twenty minutes ago. I glanced at my iPhone; it was time to call Triple A, but the phone was dead too. Its one red battery bar hadn't fazed me when I left Spago. Great. I felt like Eeyore.

"It could rain today." What was next? A rabid coyote? I was going to have to hike down the canyon in Manolos on a quest for a gas station and carry a little red plastic can back up to fill the old gal's thirst. Maybe my Nikes were still in the trunk. I wouldn't make it in those red satin stilts. I never wore heels, but I was on a date and everyone said you had to wear them. It's sexy and guys like it. I'd rather rock motorcycle boots than hobble along looking like a fool. It felt like rusty nails were digging into the tips of my toes. I'd borrowed the Manolos from my friend Jen, so I didn't think she would appreciate it if I scaled a mountain in her twelve-hundred-dollar shoes. This guy wasn't even worth it. Another asshole from Tinder. He squashed my one glimmer of hope five minutes in.

"Why are you still single? You must be a nightmare." Should have swiped *nope*, again.

I rummaged in the trunk, sifting through a Home Depot bucket. A few bottles of Cheer had toppled onto some Trader Joe's bags, and thank God, the Nikes rested by the spare tire. Wait, Nike. Shit, there was only one. I sat in the backseat and took off the Manolos. My feet were finally free, and I rubbed them to flatten their twisted crimson nubs. I laced up the one Nike and pulled on my navy UCLA sweatshirt. One ratty gym sock from underneath the floor mat was now on the other foot. I smelled like my beagle, Daisy, and looked ridiculous, but I didn't care. I found a flashlight in my earthquake kit. My pops had given it to me for Christmas, and I'd thrown it in the old gal's trunk. I had no room in my kitchen pantry; too many cans of garbanzo beans and bottles of Windex. I never thought I would open it, but it came in pretty handy that night.

My pops always told me to pay attention to the details, not to let the important stuff slip through the cracks. "You need to be a responsible young lady. You are thirty-two and a full-fledged adult." But I had a tendency to forget. I couldn't help it. My house keys, writing a rent check on time, and, well, running out of gas. This wasn't the first time. I could just see him clicking his tongue and shaking his head, his hairy gray eyebrows twitching. Last September

I puttered along on gas fumes on the 110/101 interchange. I was a "SigAlert," and drivers honked and gave me the finger as I sat stalled in the middle lane.

"Elizabeth Olivia Harrison, really, again."

I pretty much locked myself out of my apartment weekly. I learned how to jimmy the front screen by yanking on the wooden frame and sliding it upward. It rumbled and jerked, flaking white paint chips into my hair. I wrote countless reminders in blue ink on my palm, but it smudged into a blurry haze. Oh well.

Coldwater's asphalt was jagged and crumbly. It was steep like Runyon, but not as rocky. My ankles gave a bit when I stumbled on the uneven pavement. It wasn't easy with just one sneaker. Cars whizzed past, and I watched as their sparkly taillights rounded each corner and disappeared into nothingness. I thought of trying to hitch, but figured with my luck, a kook would kidnap me and drive to Tijuana to sell me as a sex slave. *No bueno.*

I decided to skip, make light of it, and have fun. This could be a great adventure. Lots of fancy people lived on Coldwater. I heard Tom Hanks had a house up here, and it was Emmy week. Who cares about that old frat guy from Tinder? He had a piece of kale stuck in his front tooth the whole time anyway.

"Well, it's a marvelous night for a Moondance with the stars up above in your eyes, a fantabulous night to make romance, hmm, hmmm."

I couldn't remember the rest of the words, and I was singing out of tune. My skipping was pretty bouncy, and I was focusing on how high I could jump in the tight leather skirt, but my shoelace caught the tip of a pothole and launched me into the brush. I was now sprawled flat with the flashlight on top of my chest; a perpendicular spotlight shot skyward. I had just gotten hockey-checked by the asphalt. The grass was damp, and my left ankle tingled. My lone sock, black and torn. It stank. I was probably lying on top of a steaming pile of shit.

"Good job, Lizzie," I muttered to myself. I sat up and dusted off the foliage and spiky branches. The foul smell was getting stronger, and the reeds rumbled. I shined the flashlight towards the swishing.

It sounded like a cat or dog was trying to make its way through. I squinted and it got closer rather quickly. Its black-and-white bushy tail poked upright, and its beady eyes glowed. It hissed, stamped, and scratched the dirt, kicking some of it up. I tiptoed away, but it was too late. The skunk's hiss became shriller and it let loose its gassy venom, spraying the front of my shins. I staggered backwards as the varmint continued its rampage into the brush. The smell was disgusting, like raw sewage. Fuck.

How could this much bad juju happen to one person in less than two hours? It wasn't my turn for bad karma. In fact, yesterday the pregnant psychic at the car wash told me that my aura was pretty high. Good things were coming my way. She was sitting next to me waiting for her Toyota Sienna. Her big belly rested on her thighs like a gigantic beach ball, and a Yorkshire terrier yipped at her feet.

"You have a lot of light in you."

Really? So, then what the hell was all this?

"Lady, hello. Are you okay?"

I was so busy hopping up and down trying to get the skunk stench off by wiping my sweatshirt all over my shins that I didn't notice a Prius taxicab had pulled up. Its headlights glared and its muted engine purred.

"Oh, hey." I shielded my eyes from the light to get a better glimpse. "I'm okay. I ran out of gas and my phone died, so I was hiking down to get to the nearest gas station." The brilliance blinded. Was this my kidnapper? Next stop Tijuana?

"C'mon, we'll give you a ride." He waved his arms into the light like he was forming snow angels against the dark sky. "I just have to drop this customer off at a party up the street." Good, he wasn't alone. What were the chances that an international taxicab kidnapping duo drove a hybrid? Minimal, I decided.

"Okay. Thanks so much."

I limped over clutching my flashlight, purse, and stinky sweatshirt. Wait till they got a whiff of me. I slid into the backseat and clutched the edge of the door.

"Jesus, lady. What happened to you?" The customer stared, mouth agape, but then pinched his nose with his thumb and forefinger. He looked kind of familiar with a roundish face and jovial smirk. His hair was a mass of dirty blond curls, puffy and 'fro-like.

"I apologize. Not only did I go on a bad date, run out of gas, and have my phone die, but Pepé Le Pew just nailed my ankles."

The driver turned and studied me before pulling his Dodgers cap down low over his eyes. They both erupted into laughter. You know, that bellyache, uncontrollable giggle when you feel like you might pee your pants. I laughed too and gave a small snort.

"Well, that's crazy. You're actually kind of foxy underneath all that mess. Anyone ever tell you, you look like the girl from *Scent of a Woman*? Whoo-ah."

Actually, the crazy homeless guy at the Laundromat said it to me all the time. He wore a rainbow Mexican blanket with no shirt and tan chinos and shouted "Whoo-ah" every time I stuck a load in the dryer.

We merged onto Coldwater. The customer pointed at my one sneaker and shook his head. How did I know him? Barry's Bootcamp? Had we been partners one day?

"Did you go to UCLA?"

"No, I went to the New School in New York."

He was younger, I would have guessed mid to late twenties. He dressed sloppily—ripped jeans, lopsided button-up, and Chuck Taylors. Ray-Ban Wayfarers clipped to the front of his shirt.

"Emmy party?"

"You know it!" He was still plugging his nose but hummed "Slow Rider."

"Do you have a cellphone I can borrow? I could call Triple-A and be out of your hair."

"I left it at my buddy's."

"I only have radio dispatch." The driver eyed me in the rearview mirror. His forehead was wrinkly with upside-down frowns.

Oh, I get it. I didn't know him. It was Jonah Hill. That was the problem with living in Los Angeles. Famous people just looked familiar.

"15308 Coldwater." We stopped in front of a driveway surrounded by an eight-foot metal fence. It was ornate, with a fleur-de-lis at the apex.

"Well, this is me," Jonah said. "You should come in and use the phone. Triple-A can get you from here." He handed the driver a fifty from a crumpled-up wad. I lingered, clutching my stinky sweatshirt. He poked his head down and smiled.

"Whatcha doin'? C'mon, whoo-ah."

I unclicked the seatbelt and stumbled. My shoeless foot throbbed, and the sock was beginning to shred. "Your friend won't mind? I mean, I'm a total mess."

"It's cool." He punched a code into the security box, and the gate opened, whining. He motioned for me to follow. The driveway was long, with tiny candles lining each side.

"Is this a fancy Emmy party?"

"Naw, just a small gathering with friends."

I could barely squeeze my way through the front door. Loads of fashion bloggers and actresses decked out in spiked Manolo gladiators and Hervé Léger dresses huddled about. I bumped into them while they drank Moscow Mules in copper mugs. They leaned sexily and took selfies. Jonah high-fived almost everyone.

"What's up, man! Party!"

It was a beautiful home. Very modern, glass walls, stainless steel with concrete floors and black-and-white Mapplethorpe-like photos. Guests gawked, frowned, or corked their nostrils. I didn't blame them.

"Who's the chick?"

"Make-A-Wish Foundation? Is she homeless? Jonah, you are too sweet."

"She's cool; she just needs to use the phone."

He was such a nice guy. I needed to rewatch *Superbad* or maybe *Moneyball*. A few bloggers scurried, clicking their heels against the concrete, scratching it like nails on a chalkboard. I sweated and my stomach did loops like the Cyclone at Coney Island. I wanted to go home, take a shower, and crawl into bed.

"Phone's over here."

We were in the kitchen, and Jonah pointed to a cordless on the counter. It was much quieter here. The caterers were working on stacking small golden bites onto silver platters. It smelled buttery and hot. Man, I was hungry. It had been six hours since I nibbled on a cheese plate at Spago. My mouth watered. The servers and chefs ogled me too. I gave a small wave.

"My main man, Jonah!"

"What's up, Franco? Rockin' party. My friend needs to use your phone. What's your name?"

"Lizzie."

"Lizzie, nice to meet you. Wow, rough night?" Of course, it was James Franco's house. The night was getting weirder by the minute. He took two steps sideways and gave me the once-over.

"Burning Man?"

"Ha, ha. Long story involving running out of gas, falling into a ditch, and pissing off a skunk. Sorry to bother you. Thanks for letting me use your phone."

"*Mi casa, su casa.*"

He was smoking an electronic cigarette and wearing pajama pants with a Hawaiian shirt. His mirrored aviator sunglasses were pulled halfway down the bridge of his nose.

"Anyone ever tell you that you look like that girl from *Scent of a Woman*?"

"Totally. I said the same thing." Jonah nodded. I was beginning to hate that movie.

"We're going to get a cocktail. You want one?" James said.

"No, thanks. I appreciate it though." I cradled the receiver.

Jonah and James strolled into the starlet jungle. I turned and the entire catering staff was still staring. I twisted my back and dialed Triple-A. The counter was lined with quirky doodads, mostly adorable Limoges boxes. One ornate teakettle, an orange tiger, and a perfectly robust beehive. I didn't envision James Franco as a collector of expensive French junk. They were lined up neatly one after the other, a gigantic mob of them. They didn't seem to go with the overall modern décor, but I guess it was kitschy. Maybe that was the point?

I picked up the beehive, listening to Neil Diamond on hold. I ran my fingers along its smooth surface. It had a tiny gold clasp, and I mindlessly fiddled to see what was inside. Maybe a swarm of adorable bumblebees? It was so delicate and yet difficult to pry open. The honeycomb top jolted off and flicked into my palm. Neil still blasted into my right ear. I scrambled, placing the top back on by cupping my palms and then gently placing it on the counter. It wobbled a smidgen but remained intact.

"Yes, I'm at 15308 Coldwater. Fifteen minutes. Thank you." I returned the receiver and took a few steps back. I needed to get out of here.

"Señorita. *¿Puedo audarle?*" The housekeeper tapped my right shoulder. I glanced at the tiny beehive.

"*Que descuidado te vez. Te estoy mirado. Compórtate, o le llamo a la policía.*" Her chocolate eyes glossed over, and she crossed her arms in front of her chest. She had a unibrow. I didn't speak Spanish, but I caught "*policía.*"

"Um, no, *gracias*. I'm going to wait...um, you know." I smiled real toothy and did a curtsy before sprinting outside.

The pool was a bottomless midnight blue. Only a handful of guests were hanging outside lounging on lawn chairs. I glanced at my wristwatch; it was 2:15 a.m. and still muggy out. I could feel the frizz puffing my hair into a hefty storm cloud. The brilliant moonlight made the water twinkle like a thousand tiny diamonds. It was relaxing and inviting, hypnotizing even. I shuffled my way around its kidney maze, inhaling the pungent chlorine. It smelled fresh and shiny. No more skunk stench. I was concentrating on how many gulps of clean air I could take in that I didn't notice the drunken fashion blogger. She staggered in her Manolos and elbowed me in the back, striking me right between the shoulder blades. I splashed head first into the shimmering liquid. It was muted and hushed under the water, calm and serene. I wanted to remain submerged and surrender. Okay, Mercury in retrograde, you win. I floated to the surface and laid on my back, arms and legs splayed out wide. My pinkie toe tingled in the tattered sock. The water was lovely and almost made me forget my predicament. That's it, turning over a new leaf. Detail and precision would be my new name. No more Lizzie.

"Hey, are you okay?"

I drifted to the edge, sopping wet, but at least I didn't smell like a skunk anymore.

"Yeah, icing on the cake."

A guy in a crisp white button-down dangled a towel. The moonlight encircled him in a glittery mist. He had sandy brown hair that hung loose over his cobalt eyes. He winked and flashed perfect movie star teeth. Did I know him? Maybe he went to that Whole Foods on Santa Monica? Boy, he was handsome.

He offered me the towel and took my hand, leading me up the pool's staircase. His hands were soft but manly. Goosebumps.

"You're even pretty wet."

"Thanks." My cheeks heated up to a blazing lilac. Maybe the car wash psychic was right?

"What's your name?"

"Elizabeth." I said elongating the "e."

"Hey, anyone ever tell you that you look like the girl from *Scent of a Woman*? Whoo-ah."

THE HOST

◇◇◇◇◇◇◇◇◇◇◇◇◇◇◇◇◇◇◇◇◇◇◇◇◇◇◇◇◇◇

The refrigerator was filled to the brim with every condiment you could imagine. Mustard, ketchup, horseradish, Catalina, Thousand Island, pickles both sweet and sour, Mr. Chow's soy sauce, crusty old ranch dressing, Italian with the oil and vinegar separated, green olives with shiny red pimentos, and a half-eaten jar of Jif peanut butter.

Emily pulled each one and placed them into a black garbage bag. She was cautious not to toss for fear they would shatter into tiny fragments, forcing the sticky contents to ooze out. The bag got quite heavy after the eighth bottle clanked its way in. She tied the top into a thick double knot. It was wrinkled, shiny, and made a lovely bow. It would take at least two more bags to clear the rest. She slammed the refrigerator door shut. The light from the icebox had illuminated the kitchen, which was now pretty much dark. Emily could hear the quiet hum from the ceiling fan above. She glanced over to the oven, where she could make out the outline of Little Debbies on the inside. Her grandmother Zellie stockpiled cookies. Lack of storage space and easy access.

"Emily, are you almost done?" Zellie asked.

Zellie's white curls peeked out from the living room. They were extra puffy and robust, frozen after being freshly sprayed with Aqua Net. The condo was tiny; it was hard to not hear whatever was going on at the other end. Zellie was the night watchman. She never missed *Dynasty* or *Dallas*, drinking tea and snacking on Hershey's Kisses till midnight. Then Emily's grandfather Elliott was up at 4 a.m. making a cereal-banana concoction while shuffling his slippers on the linoleum. You only got four hours of shut-eye on the living room pullout.

"I think I might have to make one or two more trips," Emily said.

She picked up the garbage bag and slung it over her shoulder. A few of the bottles knocked together like champagne glasses clinking at a wedding reception.

Zellie gazed out the window. Her wrinkly index finger pulled up one of the blinds. Her right hand was on her hip, and she wore a T-shirt that engulfed her tiny frame. Bony knees and varicose veins popped out just below the bottom of her pale pink Bermuda shorts. She had knee socks pulled up tight, and she kept her lavender sunglasses on even though the sun was setting. A few rays fought their way through, creating stripes across the sofa.

"What's he doing down there? Go check on him, Emmy."

"Sure, Zellie. I'll check on my way to the dumpster."

In the hall, Emily passed by the yellow velvet lamp with dangly crystals and glanced at the 1940s wedding photo of Zellie and Elliott. It looked weathered and vintage, like from a classic black-and-white film. Elliott was in a military uniform, and Zellie had perfect finger waves in her hair and a dark shade of lipstick.

Emily opened the door and staggered down the white wooden staircase, pausing halfway to watch Elliott pace in the parking lot. Each step was slow and methodical. He walked with purpose and direction. Elliott wore a baby blue floppy garden hat and pants to match. His shirt was a sunny yellow, and Emily could see that his hands were clasped behind his back. She continued on and waved.

"Hi, Grandpa." She readjusted her grip on the bag. The bottles persisted with their loud clanking.

"Hi, Emmy." He smiled and followed her towards the dumpster. "Did I tell you the one about the bagels being holy?"

"You sure did."

"What about the one with the judge?"

"Maybe not that one?"

Emily heaved the bag into the dumpster and turned. It was quite hot out. So much so that heat fumes radiated off the pavement. She had heard every one of his corny jokes a million times, and she didn't have the heart to not let him sneak one in. Elliott's blue eyes twinkled and he held his belly tight. He began to speak quietly, but his voice grew louder as he reached delivery.

"Fine, fifty dollars! That's what the judge said!" He giggled and tossed his head back.

"That's a good one." She smiled and studied him. He looked like he always did. Plump with a rosy hue. Not an ounce of cynicism or negativity. He patted his tummy and shook it.

"How do you like my Jell-O?"

"Oh, Grandpa, you are too funny. Whatcha doing?"

Emily linked her arm into his. They began to walk on the path he was previously pacing. She could see Zellie out of the corner of her eye watching from above.

"I was looking for that purple trike that Zellie used to ride, but I can't seem to find it." He scratched his temple.

Zellie hadn't ridden that gigantic trike in over twenty years. She used to cart Emily and her brother, Tom, around the parking lot. They would take turns sitting in the large metal basket, and she would peddle them in circles, humming as she went along.

"Grandpa, that's been gone for years. I think you sold it to the Rosens a long time ago." She frowned.

Elliott's eyes sparkled and he widened them a bit. He furrowed his brow and wrinkled his nose.

"I was sure it was right by the parking spot."

Emily patted his back, running her hands along his scratchy polyester polo. They continued to walk. Their pace remained leisurely but was still on a perfect path.

"How about we go to Legal Seafood for dinner when we are done cleaning up?"

Elliott stopped and put his hands on his hips. "Only if I can be the host, Emmy. It's not right if you don't let me be the host."

"Don't be silly. I want to treat."

"I'm the host."

He stamped his foot on the pavement. Emily nodded. He shook his head, satisfied with the outcome, and they started walking back and forth again. She would slip the waiter her credit card and he would never know the difference. He stopped once more. She saw a tear trickle down his wrinkled, rosy cheek.

"Sally, are we in Boston or Florida? I know I have been here. It looks so familiar; I just can't remember."

He dabbed at the tear and began to meander in circles. Sally was Elliott's youngest daughter. Emily blew out a long breath and closed her eyes. Her stomach felt empty and shallow, like a dry riverbed. She wanted to cry, but held her breath tight. She didn't want to scare him. She watched as he continued to walk in loops, round and round.

"Grandpa, let's go upstairs. I think it's almost time to go to dinner, and I promise you can be the host."

He looked up. Eyes vacant and hollow. The many wrinkles beneath were layered and deep-set. They formed geometric shapes and mazes to nowhere. Emily took his hand. She could feel the years on his weathered palm. He smiled and they climbed their way up the wooden staircase.

"I have lived here a long time."

Emily nodded.

"Do I still live here?"

Elliott surveyed the name of the building, Tilford K, at the top. His breathing was labored. He then faced the front door and began to trace "222" with his left pointer finger. Emily turned towards the courtyard. She clutched the railing and closed her eyes. She could smell the honeysuckles in bloom, and it reminded her of better times. Times when Elliott knew where he was, made his bicep muscle dance to a silly song, and argued with her about lugging her fifty-pound suitcase off the baggage carousel at the Fort Lauderdale airport. Emily smiled thinking of little old him trying to drag that suitcase out of his lime green Cadillac. He had a small dolly in the trunk, which he fabricated with bungee cords and a wire basket from the local A&P.

"Come on, Grandpa. Let's go in."

Zellie was sitting on the couch pretending to wrap up her delicate English china, but Emily knew that she had just rushed over from watching at the window.

"Zellie! There's my bride." Elliott opened his arms and walked towards her to give a big hug, but she waved him off and continued to wrap up a pink flowered teacup. "Emily, I am going to send you all the teacups. We won't have room for them at Rustling Pines."

"What's Rustling Pines?" Elliot said.

Zellie looked at Emily and glanced down. She continued to pack. "Elliott, we are moving to Rustling Pines. The movers come in two days. Emily came to help, and Gloria comes tomorrow. Remember?"

"But we live at Tilford K 222. Why are we moving?" He trailed off and went into the kitchen. Emily could hear him open the oven and sneak out a Little Debbie. Zellie shrugged and shook her head. "It's useless. He can't remember much these days."

Elliott sauntered in eating a Devil Square. He had chocolate crumbs on his chin. "A Little Debbie, a Little Debbie," he sang. He sat down in his worn leather recliner and stretched out horizontally. He moved from side to side trying to get comfy.

"You're going to spoil your appetite, Grandpa. We are going to Legal Seafood. Remember?" He ignored her and searched for the remote.

"Is it time for Dan Rather?" He glanced at his gold wristwatch. Emily didn't have the heart to tell him that Dan Rather hadn't delivered the news on CBS in years.

"Not yet."

Zellie continued packing while Elliott picked up *The Miami Herald*. He thumbed through the pages, licking his forefinger before he flipped to another section.

The condo looked sparse and sterile. Boxes surrounded them and only a few keepsakes remained untouched. The candy dish where Zellie used to leave tiny treats, a photo of Emily's mom, Gloria, and her aunt Sally in large hoop skirts from the 1950s, a small ceramic sculpture of a colonial couple dancing, and a painting of Zellie in her youth standing on a hill with bright fall foliage. Emily began to get nostalgic for her youth, for the spring breaks she spent visiting Tilford K. They played shuffleboard at the clubhouse, swam in the pool, and went on adventures investigating missing items. Elliott hid pocket watches, Indian-head coins, or his cowboy bolero and demanded a formal investigation. They crawled on their hands and knees with magnifying glasses and detective hats. When they found the treasure, he would shout, "Aha! Mystery solved!"

But they hadn't gone on adventures in years, and Emily wasn't even sure if he remembered. She was in Florida for a three-day shift. It was all she could get off from work. It was lonely. Hanging with people in their eighties reminded her of early-bird specials and funerals. She tried to remain positive by reminiscing over old photos, but it was getting harder to hold it together. She would leave Tilford K at 7 p.m., because both Zellie and Elliott went to bed early now. She picked up mac and cheese and green beans from Boston Market and sat in her crappy hotel room watching reruns of Andy Griffith on cable. Emily lay flat in the middle of the floor and wondered what it felt like to slowly lose your mind. Maybe it was like being trapped underwater not knowing which way to swim to the surface? It made her want to vomit. Her stomach churned and she cried to herself before she went to sleep. Emily wished it were like the old days, but it wasn't and never would be again.

"Maybe we should think about leaving for dinner?"

Zellie finished taping up another delicate saucer.

"I think it's best if we stay in tonight. I have that leftover meatloaf, and you have to get up early for your flight tomorrow. We don't want to bother you any more then we already have."

She stood up and took two steps into the kitchen. Emily followed and Elliott continued reading. Zellie rummaged in the refrigerator and took out a large bread pan with a crinkled piece of tinfoil covering it.

"But Zellie, I want to take you to dinner. I know how much you love the salmon. I won't let him be the host, don't worry."

"It's very sweet of you. It's just too much right now. Why don't you come back after we are settled and then we can go? I'm worried about the move and Elliott. You never know what kind of state he will be in." She pulled the tinfoil off and took the Little Debbies out of the oven.

"Go back to the hotel and relax. Order room service and rest up for your flight. I would love you to stay for dinner, but this is all we have and you don't eat meat. I might have some deviled eggs."

"That's okay, Zellie. Are you sure? Do you want to go someplace else? Maybe the Olive Garden?"

"No, baby doll. You're my sweet angel. Your mom will be here tomorrow to help us do the rest." Zellie halted her preparations and gave Emily a hug. She kissed her on the cheek. Her lips felt cracked and dry.

"Such a beauty," she mumbled and gave her a little tap on the bum.

"Elliott, Emily is leaving," Zellie hollered.

Elliott laid the paper down on the side table and stood up. He rocked back and forth, heels grazing the recliner. Emily took one last glance around the old place. She breathed in to memorize the aroma. It was a combination of chicken soup and Irish Spring.

"Where are you going, Emmy? Back to Connecticut?"

"No, Grandpa. I live in California now. Remember? We haven't lived in Connecticut for fifteen years."

"I used to grow the biggest zucchinis in Connecticut. The size of baseball bats." He was happy and smiling.

"I remember," Emily said. She squeezed him. He was a tad shorter than she recalled, and what was left of his white hair brushed against her chin.

"Okay, guys, this is me leaving. I love you."

Zellie waved and blew a kiss, and Elliott followed Emily out.

"Elliott, Emmy is leaving. You can't go with her."

He ignored her and continued on. They got to the entryway just outside 222 and Emily faced him. He was beaming, and the orange porch light from above illuminated his crinkled face and wire-rimmed glasses.

"I know you." He grabbed her pinkie finger and kissed her on the cheek and whispered, "I'm the host."

"You sure are. I love you, Grandpa." A few tears escaped and were now streaming down her face.

He let go of her pinkie, and Emily descended. She felt him watching her as she made her way down. When she got to the car he was gripping the porch railing, still staring. Emily waved and he blew a kiss. She fiddled with the car key, scratching it along the metal frame. Her hands shook like leaves gusting in the wind. Emily turned the engine on and cranked the A/C up to full blast. The cool air blew her hair every which way, but she didn't care. The tears flowed freely now, and she could still see him gazing at her as she drove out of the parking lot of Tilford K for the very last time.

THE MADNESS OF FIREFLIES

◇◇

George's footprint made an excellent pattern in the mud. Lines from her sneakers crisscrossed, creating exact definition with no mush. She loved how one hard stamp could control all that chaos. It stank bad though. She had to hold her nose with her thumb and index finger. The smell was thick and rank, like rotten garbage. George coughed twice, but then pursed her lips together to give a quiet whistle. The yellow grass swayed, and she could see Pepper making his way through. He wagged his tail, dog tags jingling. He reeked of mud, but with a tinge of sea salt. Pepper sat down next to her and began to lick the backs of her ears.

It was a beautiful June night. George could make out most of the constellations, and if she concentrated hard enough she could hear the distant crash of the waves against the seashore. It was still quite warm even though it was pretty much pitch black out. The humidity and heat had made her red curly hair uncontrollable, and she had a constant layer of moisture across her face. She'd been to the marshes a few weeks back when she followed Daniel, but he was too fast to keep up with. As he got farther and farther she tried to sprint, but eventually he disappeared into the golden straw. George meandered for hours looking for him, but that's how she happened upon Clementine.

Clementine had taken up residence in an abandoned lifeguard station. It had been pushed up the beach to the tip of the marsh. The wood was a faded baby blue with patches of tan. The paint had worn off in many sections and was cracked and splintering. George spotted the lifeguard shack as she tried to make her way home. She was steaming mad at Daniel for not letting her come with him. She was old enough; she had just graduated from the eighth grade. He could be a real pain sometimes, and besides he was only two years older than her.

It was a quarter past eight when she eyed tiny lights glimmering from that ramshackle tower. She tiptoed over with Pepper prancing three feet behind. George had a tiny Maglite that lit the path. Random bits of debris and shiny rocks littered the trail. The station was illuminated with multiple candles, and Clementine was fiddling with various Mason jars on the front shelf. Her blonde hair was piled into a messy updo, and she had a coating of dirt along her chin. Her skirt was filthy and torn in the lower-left corner, and she wore a large gray sweatshirt that consumed her tiny frame. George stared at her from fifty paces away. They hadn't seen or heard from Clem in over a year. She was startled and yet not surprised that Clem was camped out here, looking like hell. She pretty much looked the same except for the deep bags underneath her emerald eyes and all that grime.

George stood there for a good ten minutes wondering what Papa or Daniel would do, and tried to gather up her courage.

"It's no big deal; who cares?" she said to herself.

Her stomach was knotted up in thick lumps. She wanted to cry, but there were no more tears. She was like a hollowed-out piece of driftwood, empty and parched. Papa would kill her if he knew what she was about to do, but this was an opportunity she just couldn't pass up. It had been a year after all.

George didn't want to frighten her. You never knew which version of Clem you would get. She shuffled along the sand until she reached the ramp. The wood let out tiny groans as she climbed. Clem didn't even hear her; she was too busy with her Mason jars. There wasn't much else in the tower. An old wool blanket, a straw beach bag filled with rags, and some pried-open cans of Campbell's tomato soup.

"Hi," George mumbled.

Clementine twisted around. She tilted her head to the side and looked George up and down.

"Well, hello there, darlin'." She smiled and put her hands on her hips. Her chapped lips were split and peeling, and George could see thick navy bruises on the backs of her wrists.

"That's a mighty fine dog you got there. What's his name?"

"Pepper."

Pepper panted, and the candlelight irradiated some chunks of mud that caked up his caramel fur.

"My name is Clementine." She twirled her skirt, puffing it into a full parachute and picked up a Mason jar.

"Hi, Clementine. My name is George."

"George? That's a funny name for a pretty girl like you."

"My full name is Georgia Ruth, but everyone calls me George."

Clementine nodded and sat down on a bench; she stroked a jar lovingly. She didn't seem disoriented or agitated, but she didn't recognize George either. She was on another planet. She hummed and studied the Mason jars again. George concentrated on her bright green eyes. She tried to peer into them to see if there was any sparkle, but as she focused all she saw was endless desolation.

George clutched her tummy. This was typical; she didn't know why she thought it would be any different. They had spent years trying to get Clem help before she disappeared. George used to hide in her closet fastening on earphones and blasting her Walkman to a high decibel. Duran Duran blared, but she could still hear the faint screams and sound of furniture crashing. She gripped her knees tight. Tears trickled onto her sneakers, and Pepper scratched at the door.

"What's in the Mason jar?"

Clementine grinned and held it up to the ebony sky.

"Magic," she said. "Be patient and you will see."

The jar looked totally empty. It was clear with a polished gold cap and nothing inside. This was new, even for Clementine. George smiled and continued to watch the empty jar. Clem nodded and hummed.

"Look, there it is!"

The jar glowed and tiny dots flashed and glittered before quickly going dark again.

"Ah, fireflies," George said.

"Magical." Clem was beaming.

She grabbed another jar from the shelf and placed them both on the railing. She danced and picked up one of the soup cans and drank it with the metal cap still attached by one lone thread.

"Fireflies are special. They talk to each other with their light. It's how they love. I've been collecting them for a month. They protect me from you know who." Clementine dipped her index finger into the soup can to scrape out any remaining liquid. A thin tomato stain rimmed her mouth.

"Who do you need protection from?"

"The men in dark suits from the Drexal building downtown. They have been watching me for some time, but I lost them a few weeks ago. The fireflies helped, but I won't let them catch me. I have them all figured out." She clinked two of the Mason jars together.

George shook her head. She was petting Pepper and caught a hold of a wet chunk as she scratched behind his ears. Clementine was worse, but it didn't make George feel anything. She was numb. She wanted to be angry or sad, but the pit in her stomach was just starving, like she hadn't eaten for weeks. She gripped the wooden railing and watched Clementine as she busily stacked and restacked those Mason jars. It was like George wasn't even there. Why did she even bother?

She tugged on Pepper's collar and started to creep down the rickety blue incline.

"You used to love it when I made strawberry-rhubarb pie. You could eat two whole pieces with a gigantic scoop of vanilla bean ice cream."

George hesitated midstride.

"You would try on my blue flowered party frock with the gold clip-on hoops and have a lovely tea party with Pepper. George, the sweet girl with the little boy's name."

George breathed and did a slow pirouette. Clementine's back was to her. She had draped the army blanket over her shoulders and was still stacking those damn jars. The pit in her tummy churned up waves like a hurricane at Nags Head. She felt a bit dizzy but gripped the railing firmly. Her top lip quivered and a defiant tear escaped.

"Clem?" George whispered so softly that she wasn't even sure she had said it out loud.

"Are you leaving already? It was nice to meet you, sugarplum. What was your name again? Watch out for those folks from Drexal's. They are everywhere. Will you come back and visit? The fireflies are working well so they can't find me." She was talking so fast that it sounded like gibberish.

And just like that she was gone.

"Catch you later, Clementine."

George waved even though Clem wasn't paying attention. She turned and continued down the ramp. Pepper followed with his paws tapping noisily against the wood. She was a fool. She let her get to her for a split second and she almost fell to pieces. It was confusing when Clem had those moments of clarity; it lulled you into thinking that she was actually sane, but that ship had sailed long ago.

"Idiot," George said to herself.

She kicked up a mass of sand. It briefly hovered in tiny diamond specks before plummeting to the earth.

She made it home at half past nine. Papa and Daniel were sitting in front of the TV glued to the lime green couch. They were watching *Knight Rider* and eating slices of pepperoni pizza. The box was lying lazily on the coffee table. George could smell the hot cheese, and it almost made her forget that nasty marsh odor.

"Georgia Ruth, where in God's name have you been? You stink to high heaven. Go up and take a bath, and then you can come down and have a slice. There's a half Hawaiian pie in the kitchen for you."

"Yes, Papa."

His eyes were affixed to the TV and he took a large bite. George watched as the cheese oozed out in one long, drippy streak. Daniel glared at her but said nothing. She could feel his gaze burning a hole into the center of her forehead, but she ignored him and skipped up the stairs.

George decided she would keep Clementine to herself. No sense in worrying them. It's not like anything had really changed. At least not yet. She needed more time to investigate, to suss it out. Maybe she would get through to her? Clem had remembered about the pie and the tea parties. She just needed to work a little harder. Consistency was the key.

Over the next few weeks George made several trips out to the baby blue shack, but Clementine never remembered and continued to yammer about the magic of those stupid fireflies. Her speech became more erratic with each visit, and she talked in short sentences and spun in a tizzy.

So here George was again, one last time, crouching down in the smelly, dirty marsh with Pepper. She had stuffed an old photo album in her backpack and made a PB&J sandwich for Clem. The old photos would help, she was sure of it. She snuck out, telling Papa that she was going to Charlotte's for Taco Tuesday. He just nodded and read the Sunday paper on his brown leather recliner. It was summer and as long as she was home by curfew, he didn't pay too much attention.

George hunkered down and closed her eyes. She tried to ignore the nasty stench and concentrate her energy on listening to the hush of the sea's lapping waves. It was relaxing. That empty pit in her tummy didn't ache so much.

"C'mon, Pep."

Pepper shook his wet fur, and muck flew every which way. The tower glowed a little less this time, but she could still see a few candles flickering in the distance. Her muddy sneakers imprinted that perfect pattern onto the ramp, and the moon diffused her shadow against the tower's exterior.

"Clementine?"

The candles had melted down to their tips, and the wax dripped onto the railing, leaving tiny frozen blobs. The floor was littered with a plethora of empty soup cans, but the army blanket and straw bag were missing. One lone Mason jar sat dead center.

George sunk to her knees as her hands shook fiercely. Pepper put his head in her lap and licked her legs as she tried to control the quivering by interlocking her hands. The pit was now full, full of regret and disappointment. Nausea washed over her, so she blew out several elongated breaths until the air bubbled up into high-pitched hiccups.

"George, it's all right. She was never going to stay. You know what she's like. It's not really her."

George turned to see Daniel at the top of the ramp. He was holding a flashlight, and the hot wind blew his hair in a westerly direction. He smiled and nodded.

"You knew she was here?"

"Yep, the whole time."

"But why doesn't she love us?"

"Oh, George, in her own weird way, I think she does. But you gotta let her go. The person you are searching for isn't there anymore."

He stepped towards her and crouched down.

"Yeah. I guess so." She sniffled.

"I love you, George. C'mon, I'll take you to Soundview for a double scoop. My treat." He patted her back lightly and tugged at a curl underneath her right ear.

"Okay. Can you give me a minute?"

"Sure thing. Take your time. C'mon, Pep."

Daniel stood up, snapped his fingers, and Pepper followed him down. George remained on her knees and listened for their descent. She picked up the lone Mason jar and studied it. Her tears had dried up, and she was able to regain her breath although she still had the hiccups.

"Oh, Mama."

George hugged the Mason jar tight. She held it against the moonlight and watched as the tiny black dots buzzed about. The jar was cool despite the heat, and the glass felt refreshing on her warm palms. She unscrewed the golden cap and gently pulled it off. The fireflies sailed out one by one, and she watched as they brilliantly twinkled for a brief instant before going completely dark and then disappearing forever.

DIAMOND IN THE ROUGH

◇◇◇◇◇◇◇◇◇◇◇◇◇◇◇◇◇◇◇◇◇◇◇◇◇◇◇◇◇◇◇◇◇◇◇

For Ellen

Round these parts, folks don't take too kindly to gunslinging sharpshooters, particularly of the lady variety. A scarce few were scattered about, but local gossip and tiny whispers traveled far on the new frontier. Jessie Lynn Porter cocked her head westward and squinted with one eye shut when she snapped back the barrel. Rusted tin cans chimed and sailed into the tall grass. She pretty much nailed it every time. The dings sang out a cheerful ditty.

"Such a waste of talent," Pappy said.

It wasn't ladylike to swing a pistol, wear pants, or ride a horse, but Jessie Lynn didn't care. She wasn't much of a lady anyhow. She spat into the dry, cracked dirt.

"Remember to steady your back leg when you pull the trigger. Dig that boot deep."

Pappy paced when she practiced. Two steps, three steps, and then back to two. They had to go out past the barn to where the yellow grass grew mighty and steep. It smelled of sweet honeysuckle and vanilla. Jessie Lynn closed her eyes for a peep and inhaled deeply before pulling the trigger. The tin can rocketed skyward but then plummeted. Bo barked and chased it, the grass quaked as he leapt. Silly pup.

"That's enough for today, young lady. We shouldn't even be out here. Your mama would have my head. God rest her soul."

He always said that, but then they were back at it after he got home from a trip. Pappy rode for the Central Overland California and Pikes Peak Express. He left from Hollenberg Station, which was just around the bend, and was gone for a little more than a week. Pappy was the best rider she'd ever seen. Quick and elegant, a deafening blur against the cobalt sky.

"Yes, sir." Jessie Lynn offered him the pistol. He twirled it for a spell before settling it into the holster.

"Let's go and see what Granddad cooked up for supper."

He clapped his weathered palms against the chaps. Smudges of dust dotted his neckline, and he removed his hat and shook it. Flecks of silver shimmered in his hair. The sun started to sink into a hazy burnt orange.

"You need to do ladylike things, and shootin' ain't one of them. Should have left you in Philadelphia with Uncle Jack and Aunt Charlotte."

She nodded. No use in arguing with him.

Jessie Lynn preferred Kansas to Philly. At least she thought she did. They traveled across the frontier when she was ten years old, and now she was seventeen, so that was a ways back. Philadelphia was grimy and loud. Horseshoes clopped on the pavement and she had to wear a dress with a petticoat, which was itchy and hard to walk in.

"Sit up straight, chew with your mouth closed, hush up."

Too many rules. She didn't understand how ladies endured it.

Kansas was serene. She loved the fluffy cottonwoods, especially in autumn, when the leaves turned a golden shade of amber. Pappy let her wear pants in Kansas, because no one was around for miles. Granddad didn't care for it too much, but he let her be. It was quiet as a whisper except for the wind blowin' and the steady gallop of Pappy's horse when he returned. Sometimes she could catch the drumbeat from the Pawnee or glimpse their smoke plumes, but it was pretty faint.

"I'm quite peckish. Hope he made stew."

"Me too. Just makes my mouth water."

She licked her chops and whistled.

"C'mon, Bo."

Bo leapt, crunching a crooked path in his wake. It was a good long walk back to the cabin. There wasn't much to see except a few of those cottonwoods and an ocean of grass. It swished and parted as she trudged. Jessie Lynn imagined it like the Red Sea splitting in two.

"You leaving soon?"

"Think so. Maybe day after tomorrow."

"Any chance I can come with? I promise to be no trouble. You won't even know I'm there."

Pappy paused. She could see tiny beads of sweat trail down his back as his shoulders crept up to his ears.

"Jessie Lynn, you know the answer to that. Now quit asking me."

She yanked a piece of grass and dangled it from her bottom lip.

"Fiddlesticks."

Pappy continued walking.

"Silly girl," he muttered.

But she wasn't silly. Not even a tiny bit. She could ride a horse pretty good. In fact, better than most of those sissy boys in town, and she could certainly outshoot them, but that wasn't common knowledge. She had to act like a lady in public or Pappy would tan her hide.

"Evening, Granddad."

Granddad was hunched over the stove, clanking a bulky blue pot. Wisps of white hair hung loose over his eyes.

"Evening. You two done with that nonsense?"

"It's not nonsense."

She regretted it once the words had escaped into the heavens and scratched at his ears, but it was too late. She could see him wince.

"Sure is, little lady. Shooting tin cans. For what?" He shook the wooden spoon at her.

"It's good practice. I have a talent for it. Pappy says so."

"So, are you going be the next Hollenberg Station sheriff? Poppycock. Shooting a tin can and shooting a man is totally different."

"All right, that's enough. It's good for her to know how just in case. It can get mighty lonely out here with just you two. Come on now, let's eat."

Granddad waved them off and went back to stirring. He worried that she would never catch a husband with her wild ways. What kind of man wants a wife who can't cook and shoots better than him? Seemed awful backwards.

"Jessie Lynn, my sweet diamond in the rough."

Pappy patted her on the back and gave her a tight squeeze.

"You be you."

Pappy left the next day. It was a crisp November morning. Frost coated the tips of the yellow grass like crystal fragments. He had to ride all the way to Fort Kearny. News of the election had come. He swung the Mochilla over the saddle and hopped on. Lucky was a good steed. Magnificent and dark like midnight. A patch of white fur ran down her forehead till it reached her muzzle. Pappy tapped the sides of the Mochilla, double-checking for his pistol, canteen and, most important, the mail. A shiny bugle was draped from his neck.

"Be a good girl. Mind your grandfather." His eyebrows were strewn with flecks of snow, and his mouth was a tad bluish.

"Heya!"

He kicked Lucky's girth with his heel, and she took off. Jessie Lynn stood on the porch swathed in a wool blanket studying them until they vanished. It was just after 6 a.m., and Granddad was still asleep. She needed to hurry if she didn't want to get too far behind. Of course he'd said no, but she was going anyway. He wouldn't be upset when he saw that she could do it. He would be proud; she beamed just thinkin' about it.

She sprinted to the barn. Her satchel was already affixed to Lucy. She had snuck out last night after everyone was sound asleep. Bo trailed and yelped.

"Hush. You'll wake Granddad."

Lucy wasn't as quick as Lucky, but she would get the job done. Jessie Lynn patted her hip; the pistol was nice and snug.

"I'll be back before you know it." Bo tilted his head and whimpered.

"Giddyup!"

Lucy trotted and picked up speed as she reached the edge of the yellow grass. Kunuk would join her one mile south of the Pawnee village. She had met Kunuk while she was practicing in the woods six months ago. Pappy was on a trip, and Kunuk surveyed her from atop a cottonwood. He wasn't hard to miss. Tall and lean, skin covered in charcoal-tinted tattoos. She was afraid he was going to shoot her with his bow and arrow, but he just watched from above and cheered when she hit a can.

"Kakow!"

When Pappy was away, Kunuk taught her to use the bow and arrow and to speak with her hands, and she tried to teach him how to shoot. He spoke English pretty well, and they became fast friends. Frankly, he was her only friend. He was so wild and free, and she was too.

Jessie Lynn spotted Kunuk up ahead. His horse the color of unblemished snow. Two red feathers poked out of his long dark hair, his bow strapped diagonally across his chest.

"Your papa rode through a few ago."

"Sorry I'm late. It was hard to leave with Bo making a commotion and all."

Kunuk steered west and took off.

"Wait for me!"

He was a better rider than she, and he didn't even have a saddle. But to be fair, he got to ride a lot more. He hunted and fished and trotted on his snow-colored pony every day. Sometimes he rode backwards just to show off.

Jessie Lynn's tummy looped round and round. This was so exciting. She was going on a regular adventure. Maybe once Pappy saw how capable she was, she could go to work too. Earn her own living. Be a professional rider just like him. Then they would be together all the time. A bona fide team.

Jessie Lynn sunk into decay, rotting like a tree stump when Pappy was gone. It was so lonely, and she was bored when Kunuk hunted with his tribe. Granddad wasn't much entertainment. All he did was cook, read books, and, well, complain about how unladylike she was. He tried to teach her how to sew and cook, but she just made a mess of things and burned the bottom of the fry pan into a black crusty heap. Jessie Lynn saw Pappy off on all his trips and waited for his return by sitting cross-legged on the front porch's bottom stoop. She never missed it, even if it was raining. The only good thing she could remember about Philly was that she saw Pappy every day, and in Kansas she didn't. Things would be different soon. She was really doing it.

Lucy's hooves kicked up chunks of snow, slapping Jessie Lynn in the face, but her eyes stayed glued to that white horse. Kunuk was an expert tracker, and she needed him. He knew all sorts of shortcuts, so they would hopefully catch up to him at Liberty Farm. They didn't have to switch horses like pappy did, but he was one of the company's best riders, so it would definitely be a challenge.

"Hey! Wait for me!"

Kunuk slowed to a trot. He tapped his fingers rhythmically against Snowy's white mane. He didn't like to wait.

"Sorry, I'm not as fast as you."

"Yes, I know." He continued tapping. "We need to hurry or we won't be able to catch him at Liberty Farm."

"I know. I'm doing my best." Jessie Lynn blew out a surge of air.

"Do better." He hooted and then took off again.

This time she didn't hesitate. Lucy lurched, almost thwacking her off, but then they sailed into a smooth glide. The wind whipped viciously, and the trees melded into a charcoal fog. She caught up to two lengths behind. The woods reeked of smoke and kindling. Folks must be getting up and prepping breakfast, which reminded her that she didn't have any. Her tummy growled, but she wasn't going to mention it. She would never hear the end of it. She licked her lips and swallowed some crispy flakes and concentrated on Kunuk's shiny red feathers. It was about all she could discern at this pace.

He whistled and decelerated.

"What's up?"

"Someone else was on this path."

He halted and indicated the fresh tracks up ahead. They formed a pattern, marking the white carpet geometrically.

"So what? I'm sure we are not the only ones who take this route. Are you hungry? 'Cause I'm famished."

"Shhhh."

He was now off his horse examining the prints, sniffing and scooping his finger into the mud.

"What are you doing?"

"Shhh."

Kunuk continued to poke around. Jessie Lynn dismounted and dug into her pack for some jerky. She ripped off a piece and chewed. It was salty but satisfying. It warmed her core as it traveled down her esophagus. She guzzled from her canteen, and drops of water clung to her chin. Kunuk arose and crinkled his nose.

"Cigar. He was smoking a cigar."

"Who was?"

"The rider."

"Why do we care? Jerky?" she offered.

He shook his head.

"Because you always need to know what is in front of you and what is behind you."

"Ah. Yes. Of course."

She wouldn't have made it this far on her own.

"Thanks, Kunuk. I don't know what I would do without you."

He tried not to smile, but the edges of his lips snuck higher. He sat up straight and adjusted his bow.

"Okay. Let's keep going."

They both hopped back on and moseyed for a spell.

"Jessie Lynn. Do you miss your mama?"

He was picking up speed and gazing up ahead.

She hadn't really thought about it for a spell. Her mama had passed on the trip out west. She caught tuberculosis, hacked up blood, and sweated profusely. Her eyes enflamed and skin a sallow ash. Jessie Lynn tried to cool her off with wet compresses as she hummed. Mama had the prettiest smile, even at the end.

"I do. I miss the way she read to me before I went to sleep. She smelled so sweet, like peonies. Do you miss your mama?"

He nodded. Kunuk didn't like to talk about how the French raided his village when he was six. They shot his mama in the forehead and murdered the rest of the women and children. Kunuk was on a hunt with his papa and the other tribesmen. They returned to find her flat, eyes open, auburn wounds splintered and parched. Flies encircled her dark braids, crowning the gory mess.

"I miss Pappy too, always on some kind of ride. Delivering letters and packages for Pikes Peak. He's exhausted when he's home, holed up in his room. He used to be hilarious. He used to laugh."

Kunuk listened. They didn't need to chatter. Their silence roared volumes.

"C'mon, we're close."

They raced on the outskirts, weaving in and out of the cottonwoods. It was still chilly despite the sun's shiny glow. The wind nipped and slunk up her spine. Liberty Farm was getting clearer. She could make out the silhouette of a dreary ramshackle structure. Smoke huffed from its squat chimney, and three steeds were parked at a hitching post out front. A handful of riders milled about. One of them must be Pappy.

Kunuk flung his palm parallel.

"We should walk from here."

He motioned for her to approach from the rear. Pappy stood at the hitching post. He was already switching horses by draping the Mochilla over a dappled pony. He was adjusting the pack and placing the horn back around his collar. Another rider was mounted twenty paces to the right, but he didn't look like a Pikes Peak fellow. He wore all black. His belly was robust and flopped over his holster as he puffed on a massive cigar.

"Kunuk, that must be the rider," she whispered.

"Shhh."

Pappy swigged from his canteen and rubbed the pony's muzzle. He jumped on.

They were close enough now that she could glimpse the outline of Pappy's shiny spurs. They stopped just behind the station. The man in black yakked with Pappy, but she couldn't make out what they were talkin' about. Their voices grew into shouts. The man in black snatched up his pistol. His mound of wiggly flesh rattled as he adjusted his stance. He aimed at Pappy.

"Hand it over, real slow like, and no one will get hurt."

"Sir, I cannot. I am on official business for Pikes Peak," Pappy said calmly.

He patted the Mochilla and sat upright. The sun was at full tilt and radiated, swathing him in a saintly shimmer.

Jessie Lynn tried to hop off, but her feet clung to the stirrups. Tears gushed out like a shattered dam.

"Pappy," she screamed.

Kunuk drew his bow.

"Jessie Lynn, what in the world..."

A thunderous boom splintered and whacked Pappy off his steed. He was now flat on his back in the snow. His left leg quivered and a crimson stream leaked onto the icy terrain. The man in black's arm was erect, pistol smoldering. He was still puffing on that stinky cigar.

Jessie Lynn wiped at the tears and took in a shallow breath. Before she knew it, her pistol was drawn. The man in black stepped over Pappy and seized the Mochilla.

"Silly girl," he muttered.

She shut one eye and cracked back the barrel. She pictured those tin cans and waited for the ding, but this time it sounded different.

The gunshot struck him right between the eyes; he teetered a bit before toppling over. The bullet met his skull with a hushed whine. She never missed, not even without the ding.

"Pappy!"

Jessie Lynn raced, skidding across the frosted roots. Her legs splayed and wobbled. Kunuk trotted after her. Pappy's eyes were still open. He was breathing heavily and clutching his chest, encircled in a red sea. She collapsed into the sticky liquid.

"It's okay, Pappy. You're fine; it barely grazed you."

She seized his hand and clasped it. It was cool and clammy.

"It's almost time for breakfast." Jessie Lynn straightened a lock of hair from underneath his hat.

"You want eggs with bacon," she continued.

"You hit 'im? In one shot?" He was half smiling; blood trickled from his tongue.

"Yes, sir."

"That's my girl. Finish it."

"What?" She looked up.

Kunuk loomed over the fat mound.

"He's dead." He kicked the hefty belly and picked up Pappy's Mochilla.

Jessie Lynn looked back down.

"Pappy."

"You're just like your mama, so stubborn, so strong. You be the rider now. I'm so proud of you." Pappy reached up to stroke her cheek. His fingers, cool like indigo daggers. He closed his eyes.

"Mind your Granddad."

His leg quake dissipated, and then he was immobile, enshrined in that crimson pool.

"Pappy, Pappy!"

She shook him a few times. But he didn't move. She sat up and caressed his hand for a minute. Blood was all over her shirt, and it matted up her dark hair.

"Oh, Pappy..."

She kissed his lifeless palm and sat quiet for a good five minutes. Then she stood up. Kunuk nodded and handed her the Mochilla.

"I love you, Pappy," she whispered, and mounted Lucy. She blew a kiss.

A few townsfolk surveyed them from their windows. She glimpsed their noses pressed up against the frosty glass. The shine from the porch's light illuminated their ghostly shadows. They needed to hurry. Granddad would certainly be worried sick by now. She saluted. Kunuk was behind her; he clenched the bugle in his fist. She patted the Mochilla just like she had seen Pappy do a thousand times, and they were off. They glided in complete silence for the last thirty miles to Fort Kearny. The wind scorched her parched tears, and the pitter-patter of the gallop was somewhat comforting. She was doing this for Pappy. And, well, for herself a bit too. Kunuk blasted the horn into a regal ode upon their arrival. They had big news to deliver. Abraham Lincoln had just been elected the sixteenth president of the United States of America.

WINK, CLICK, SWIPE

Nikki starred at the illuminated computer screen. The room was dark, but the powerful light from the monitor cast diagonal shadows along the silver keyboard. The cursor blinked like it was mocking her indecision. It was impatient and annoyed at her lack of enthusiasm. She nudged the mouse to curb its loud judgment.

"You don't know me," she said, like she could shame it into submission. It ignored her and continued with its incessant blinking.

Nikki blew out a elongated stream of air. It escaped her lips in a perfect coil but fogged up the screen. She continued to click about. She was tired. The whole process made her feel like driftwood dancing on the seashore, aimless and empty. She couldn't attach any emotion to it. All she saw were lovely photographs. Him at a wedding in Palm Beach; him with a million friends guzzling champagne on a yacht; and him traveling to Machu Picchu. It had no breath, no laughter, and no depth. It was two-dimensional and exact perfection. She felt like she was shopping for a human being on an online catalog. *I'll take Doug in a size medium.* What if he didn't fit? Or he wasn't as advertised? If his life was so incredible, why was he shopping for a mate on the internet? It really was ridiculous when you reflected on what you were actually doing.

Click. Everyone appeared so cheerful or pensive. Their lives were filled with endless hobbies and heaps of expeditions. Rugged hikers and snowboarders in shiny red helmets, photos of the Eiffel Tower in springtime, and portraits of hugs with mom or their adorable toddler nieces. There were a handful of muted scanned photos, colors saturated and creases adorning the edges. The fashions and hairstyles appeared outdated. Her left hand began to ache. Maybe she would get carpal tunnel syndrome from internet dating? She shook her wrist and cracked her rosy-white knuckles with one swift twist.

It was the digital age of perfectly Botoxed photographs. Nikki missed the '90s, when you had to go to CVS and wait a week to pick up your four-by-six prints. There was no Photoshop, filters, or instant deletion. If you had a goofy expression or red-eye, that was it. The only way to destroy the evidence was to rip it up into tiny bits. You had to live with your double chin, blurry hair, and half-closed pirate eye. It was fun to look back on those silly snapshots.

But most photographs were far from masterpieces. There were a number of out-of-focus muddled group shots, men shirtless taking selfies in bathrooms, and awkward gentlemen holding bizarre props. Guns, golf clubs, puppies, or baked goods. Creepy-scary smiles, angry eyes, and giant beefy exercise freaks pumping iron. Nikki had to click through at lightning speed, as they triggered shooting pains up the base of her spine to the tip of her neck.

She was certain they sized her up too. What was wrong with her? Why was she still alone? In fact, most of the dates she went on asked this very question.

"Why are you still single? You are very pretty."

"Why are you still single?" They were all in the same boat.

She wanted to continue with "because I keep going out with assholes like you," but she refrained. They probably thought she was old or crazy. Maybe they thought she was catfishing them?

It was just a snap evaluation. She knew she was just as judgmental, but it was difficult to gaze into the depths of something so foreign and flat. She couldn't gander into their soul or imagine the sparkle in their eyes. There was no magic, and it numbed her into a robot. She tapped her thumb against the smooth surface of the mouse. The text brought an extra-dense layer. They were searching for such odd things. If you could pull off a little black dress but rock flip-flops and denim, you fit the bill. "No drama" was a significant requirement, and there was a constant declaration of quests for BFFs or partners in crime. A few candidates had mandatory demands for knowledge of *Game of Thrones* or a love of beer pong.

Nikki just wanted to know that they were not insane. There was no point of reference or accountability. They could chop her up into a million tiny pieces, and no one would be the wiser. Right now, she would settle for a funny gentleman who wanted to go to the movies or grab a cocktail. A partner in crime was a tall order at this stage of the game. Wasn't that putting the cart before the horse?

Click. But they might be delightful, hilarious, charismatic or, most important, normal. She was. There could be a male version of her wandering the cyber universe thinking the same thing. It was like rummaging for that one shiny needle in a mountain of filthy hay.

"Be positive," Nikki repeated over and over to remain semi-engaged. She had a knee-jerk reaction to delete her profile and surrender to the notion that love and technology didn't mesh. It made her stomach swell, and the acid in her underbelly trickled up to her throat. She swallowed and continued hunting.

The profiles persisted with varied complaints and strong ultimatums. Don't message if you have a tiny puppy in your purse, are in hot pursuit of a sugar daddy, or live outside of a twenty-mile radius. Boundless inventories of what they desired and despised. What happened to the value of a genuine person, someone with a sense of humor? It appeared to be about location, diet, or your flair for fashion.

It was an endless buffet. Blondes, redheads, brunettes. Blue eyes, hazel, fit, skinny, tall, and short. It was like trying to select a slice of pizza with every kind available. Pepperoni, veggie, Hawaiian, or red onion? Oh, but wait, there was also gluten-free and bacon lover's too.

It was the bigger, better, grass-is-always greener syndrome. They pursued aggressively and moved on, pecking their way through like roosters devouring seeds at sunrise. It was a caffeine-riddled ADD existence. Most of them were weeks shy from their last entanglement, surmising you meant nothing based on timing. Dating eleven women before settling was mandatory. It was a complex mathematical computation. It didn't matter if there was connection, chemistry, or nine-hour dates. Next.

Click. Nikki didn't spot too many prospects. It was a unique happenstance to connect, to find a person of substance and quality. She had to dig deep in the messy bowels and scour high and low for that one special dude. A brilliant headlamp was required and a strong sturdy shovel to sift through layers of Sheetrock, mud, and knotty branches. Her arms throbbed from the digging. She was exhausted with search engines, algorithms, and winks. It was clinical and contrived. She couldn't squeeze herself into their perfectly constructed box no matter how hard she tried.

She repositioned the mouse and drew figure eights. The room was still pitch black except for the monitor casting its sunny glow. It left a precise spotlight over the center of the room. The cursor persisted again with its angry flashing.

"I give up. You win."

Nikki nudged the mouse along the length of the screen to select Shut Down from the pop-up menu, but just before she reached her selection a tiny white envelope appeared. She halted the advancement of the cursor and sat in silence glaring at the miniature icon. The room was silent except for the constant hum of the computer's hard drive. She could feel the delicate vibration underneath the mouse as it shook her frozen palm. She dragged the cursor over and left it blinking just below the unopened post.

Click.

CIVIL TWILIGHT

◇◇◇◇◇◇◇◇◇◇◇◇◇◇◇◇◇◇◇◇◇◇◇◇◇◇◇◇◇◇◇◇◇◇◇◇

It all started with a roll of butterscotch Life Savers. Sylvia raked her fingers along all ten tubes. They were stacked up neatly one on top of another like a perfect set of Lincoln Logs. The surface was smooth and yet bumpy as each digit traveled. Her manicured French tips hovered and dipped down before kissing the yellow wrapper. With a flick of the wrist she engulfed the roll and slid it into the left pocket of her herringbone trench. She had never intended to take the candy. Sylvia didn't even like sweets. They were terrible for your teeth, especially after seven decades of dental work.

"Be true to your teeth or they will be false to you," Murray always told the children at Halloween.

She had meant to pick up her Lipitor medication and a few bars of Dove soap, but instead wandered the aisles browsing knickknacks and apothecary items. All the Christmas hoopla was out in full regalia. Chubby Santa Claus lawn ornaments, Rudolphs with bright red flashing noses, and miniature Nativity scenes. A dreadful rendition of "Jingle Bells" droned on.

And then the candy aisle glared with its bright confections.

"Heavens to Betsy, the reason why most people are obese," Sylvia murmured.

M&Ms and Kit Kats beckoned. She contemplated a Christmas care package for Henry, but that shiny gold roll hissed and sparkled.

Before she knew it, the roll was in her pocket and she was strolling out of CVS. The butterflies remained dormant, and she moseyed in a sluggish manner. Last April she'd had her right hip replaced, and now she inched along like a tiny caterpillar.

"Goodnight, ma'am, and happy holidays," the little cashier girl shouted. Her smile was wide and full of metal. A red ribbon dangled from her long blonde ponytail.

"Happy holidays to you too, young lady."

The sliding doors clicked. The parking lot was snowy and the air felt cool, but burned a bit when she inhaled. Good thing she had worn her galoshes. They had just been hit with a terrible nor'easter three days prior. She took her leather gloves out of her pocketbook and slipped them on. They were a dusty shade of brown, but the shearling inside kept her fingers nice and toasty. Sylvia didn't feel guilty. She smiled and trudged her way through the mush, taking her steps sensibly. The last thing she needed was another broken hip.

The car's engine hummed like her sweet tabby, Muffin. The old Volvo ran pretty well but needed a few minutes to adjust to Boston's chilly December. You would think she would be used to it after living in New England for seventy years, but the winters never got any easier. Must be why Myrtle and Fred Prenovitz hightailed it down to Delray Beach to be snowbirds. Most of their friends had flown the coop. It was just the Gilberts on the other side of Newberry Lane and her that remained.

Sylvia hated winter when everyone was in the balmy sunshine. Myrtle sent postcards and letters with snapshots of shuffleboard and square dancing. She looked suntanned and smiley. Her hoop skirt was pale pink and fluffy. It was desolate and lonely in Sylvia's frozen tundra. It had been two years since Murray passed, and she still thought of him every day. The wisp of white hairs on top of his rosy freckled head, the callus on his left palm, and the way he hummed when he trimmed the hedges. They planned to be snowbirds themselves, but the prostate cancer took him before they could make the move.

Sylvia took the roll out and studied its shiny wrapper. It wasn't hard to swipe. Who would suspect an old lady anyway? She wasn't a bad person, and didn't believe in stealing. She had strict morals and went to the First Presbyterian Church on Bleeker every Sunday. No one would miss this. She was in control and alive. Most of the time she felt pretty numb.

It was like Sylvia was a hologram. She could feel people's distant gaze as they pierced beyond the center of her being. No one said "hi" as she shopped at the A&P. She smiled at the lovely toddlers getting pushed around in rickety metal carts. But their mothers plowed past at a dizzying pace, knocking her as she selected the perfect peach. She examined its yellow-orange tint and squeezed its fuzzy exterior, searching for just the right amount of bounce. She paid the thoughtless moms no mind.

Sylvia was a certifiable mess the first six months that Murray was gone. She would take a shower with the temperature turned to boiling hot. The water pounded on her back, leaving it a bright shade of plum. She wheezed, screamed, and the tears gushed out like Niagara Falls. Winded and exhausted, she would lie down for a half an hour, shivering with a towel turban wrapped around her head.

She kept the crying fits private. It wasn't appropriate to let go in public. Sylvia needed to be strong. She was the adult even though her youngest, Lara, was thirty-six. Murray had taken care of most of the details in their life. Paying the bills, fixing the dishwasher, and reminding her to take her cholesterol medication. But she managed to figure it out. It took some time but she could fake it pretty good.

The roll of Life Savers resided in the bottom-left drawer of the service porch's teak credenza. The credenza was chock-full of wedding silver and fine English china, but she rarely dipped into that. Sylvia took the prize out and studied its pearly sheen, rolling it over in her palm before returning it to its new home. Gradually, she added to the collection. Yo-yos from Walgreens, sparkly snow globes, Tic Tacs, a tube of cherry red Maybelline long-lasting lipstick, and a tiny box of screws from Laurel Hardware. She never got caught. The items fit neatly into her pocketbook or jacket's interior. The clerks were far too engrossed on their cellphones or helping other customers. She could hear their gadgets beep and buzz as she hobbled up and down the aisles. She never took anything bulky or over ten dollars. There was a system and a set of rules. Never swipe more than once a week or take a useful item. All the objects retired to the Life Saver drawer.

The loot was never displayed. It sat quietly in alphabetical order, to be eyed only by Sylvia. She beamed as she peeked inside the treasure chest. It was a wonderful silly secret. The service porch was her favorite room in the house. It overlooked the flower garden, and in the summertime the smell of hydrangeas was delicious and delightful. Murray and Sylvia had their tea here, every day at civil twilight. The horizon was so clearly defined. The illumination and colors were most spectacular when the heavens were spotless. The blushing ginger hues were saturated and brilliant. Murray would drape his arm over her shoulder and entwined his pinkie finger at the base of hers. He smelled of soap and Cuban cigars. They gazed as the sun sank into darkness. But now civil twilight made her heart deflate. She could feel each tender thump as it banged against her chest cavity. Sylvia preferred nightfall now.

Her world was silent, filled with the occasional phone call and sporadic visits from the children. Sometimes three days would pass without human contact, unless you counted the mailman, which Sylvia didn't. Slippers shuffling against the parquet, Muffin's far-off meow, and the coffee pots percolating made up her daily monotonous symphony. The closet was still full of Murray's clothes. She couldn't bring herself to donate them. They smelled of Polo aftershave, and it was comforting to inhale its woodsy odor. She buried her nose into the heart of the material to get its last lingering fragrance.

Henry was the only one who could make her forget. Her number-one grandson was such a pistol. He ruled the roost at eight.

"Don't think of me as your cousin. Think of me as your boss," Sylvia overheard Henry telling Lara's six-year-old twins. The towheaded rascals nodded and trailed him towards the old weeping willow's tire swing. He toted a jagged branch and pumped it up and down like he was the Pied Piper of the family. His tiny voice was sweet and soft, and his smile was quite sunny. He loved when she made him a half grapefruit with sprinkled granulated sugar and dotted with a shiny maraschino cherry. He gripped her hand at the funeral and stroked her tear-stained cheek.

"Don't cry, Nana. I love you."

But it had been almost nine months since she had seen Henry or any of the other grandchildren. Lara and George promised to visit more after Murray passed, but they made the trek only annually.

To pass the time, Sylvia read Tom Clancy novels and ran countless errands. Filene's Basement occupied a good three hours. The retailer in the city was the best, so Sylvia took the T to Haymarket station and walked the rest of the way to Washington Street. She passed a Dunkin' Donuts and sometimes treated herself to a hot chocolate and two glazed Munchkins. The flaky sugar on the pastry clung to her icy fingers, so she licked off every decadent drop.

The department store was warm and crowded with a plethora of tourists bundled up in puffy winter attire. They looked like Michelin Men. Sylvia tested pots and pans by clanking their tops off and on. She sampled perfumes, spraying them onto tiny sticks, waving them to and fro and drawing in their aroma. She rolled luggage, listening for squeaky wheels.

Boy, she was pathetic. Filling her days with this drivel. At least it passed the time and she was learning a great deal about consumer products. She used to have such a full life. President of the Suffolk County PTA, volunteering at the Colonial Society of Massachusetts, and tending to her prize-winning vegetable garden. Her tomatoes were to die for. They were impeccably ripe and plump, the size of tiny pumpkins and a most stunning shade of crimson. And here she was trying on sunglasses at a discount department store. Oversized purple Perry Ellis, mirrored Aviators, and big black Jackie Os. The Jackie Os didn't look half bad. They framed her face in an archetypal fashion. She tilted her head from left to right and flicked them on and off, gazing at her reflection. The dark lenses helped detract from the harsh fluorescents, which had started to give her a slight migraine. She looked mysterious and exotic in the eyewear, like a celebrity.

Sylvia heaved her pocketbook over her shoulder and tugged on her leather gloves. She shuffled out of accessories still wearing the Jackie Os. The linoleum was besieged with dirt and moisture, and tourists bumped into her.

"Ma'am, are you okay? May I help you?"

A sales clerk was standing behind her. Her spectacles were pulled down the bridge of her nose, and she had a plastic nametag that read SUSAN. Sylvia couldn't make out if she was frowning or if that was just the way her mouth swooped southbound. Her hands shook, but she clasped them together and smiled.

"Yes, dear."

Susan outstretched one scrawny arm and handed Sylvia her Burberry scarf.

"Oh my, well, thank you so much. I would forget my head if it wasn't screwed on."

"You're very welcome! Love the sunglasses. Have a great day."

"Thank you, dear. You too."

Sylvia turned and shuffled into the blistering frost. Her right hip ached as she stumbled faster than usual. The wind was quite strong, so she pulled her scarf tight and buttoned her coat to the tippy top. That was it. She had to stop. What was she doing? She could go to jail and her family would have to come and bail her out. How embarrassing. At first it was just a speck of excitement. Something small, a secret, a little harmless fun. A way to pinch herself to let her know she was still standing among the land of the living. But this was too close, plus she had diverted from the rules. The sunglasses were close to fifty dollars and she had started to swipe daily. Okay. Cold turkey. She would stop.

But she couldn't. It was habitual, and the credenza was now quite full with loads of useless trinkets. The loot was no longer organized or in alphabetical order. It was a massive heap. She needed this like she needed oxygen. Breathe in, breathe out.

George finally made good on his promise and brought Henry for a weeklong visit. It was the perfect time of year. The garden was in full bloom, and the weather was just lovely. All the snowbirds trudged their way back. She could hear them dragging their luggage off the car roofs and running the lawn mowers. She had many plans for Henry. They would go to Fenway for a Red Socks game, have a lemonade stand, and she would cook him his favorite meal: eggplant parmesan. He was such a beautiful child. Freckles dotted his tiny nose, and his red hair stuck straight up. He sang in a low whisper when he was absorbed in a task, and he never colored outside of the lines. His work was meticulous. He must have gotten that from Murray.

"Henry, George, dinner in fifteen."

Sylvia opened the oven and a blast of heat doused her cheeks. The tomato sauce was bubbling, and the cheese had a tannish sheen.

"Nana, Nana. Come here."

Sylvia shut the door and walked towards Henry's soft crooning. She tugged the dish towel over her index finger to remove some sauce. Her walk was still sluggish. That hip ache hadn't dissipated.

"Yes, dear. What is it? It's almost dinnertime. Henry, where are you?"

Sylvia froze, and the dish towel plummeted onto the parquet. The pain in her hip grew sharper. It pulsed and sputtered with a nasty sting. Henry was kneeling on the ground in the service porch bent over the bottom-left drawer of the credenza. She couldn't see his head because it was buried deep within the teak. His tiny legs jutted skyward as he rummaged. He poked his head out, shook, and contemplated a stolen treasure. The tiny bluebird sculpture, a Koosh ball, paintbrushes, and finally the gold roll of Life Savers.

"Nana, wow!" He smiled and giggled as he continued to search.

Sylvia stood still. Her hip was beginning to ache so bad that she thought she might collapse. What if George came down? How was she going to explain? She managed to slide closer using the end table and leather recliner to propel her to the porch's French doors. She gripped the door frame and squinted so Henry couldn't see the tears seeping out.

"Nana, what is this? Is this for me?" He dangled a small silver airplane ornament.

She didn't know what to say. That she was a thief, a pathetic old lady who had nothing better to do than steal and wait for her demise? Henry took the miniature airplane and stumbled, clopping his way out.

"Daddy, Daddy, look."

Sylvia clutched the door but then took one excruciating step onto the porch. She kicked the credenza drawer shut with her good leg and limped over to the daybed. Her face was now soaked with puddles of salty moisture, and she gasped to draw in fresh air. The windowpanes were wide open, and she could smell the fragrant hydrangeas. The June bugs tapped the porch's screens with deliberate aim as they went about their business. The sky was that perfect tinge of pinky-orange. She could still see patches of indigo, and there wasn't a cloud in sight. It was civil twilight now. The pain in her hip continued with its relentless banging, and her head throbbed with a chaotic rumbling. Her heart was shriveled like a crumpled piece of garbage. There was no avoiding it. Sylvia gazed up. Illumination had reached perfection. The sunset flooded the sky with its magnificent golden tones for a brief moment and then descended into the horizon, leaving her in complete darkness.

PERFUME VENGEANCE

◇◇◇◇◇◇◇◇◇◇◇◇◇◇◇◇◇◇◇◇◇◇◇◇◇◇◇◇◇◇◇◇◇◇◇◇◇◇

The smell of chalk was musty and thick. Pastel smoke doused the air, and Ellie coughed. She fished in her pail for another color and reclined on the hard wood. The dining room chair's underbelly wasn't the easiest surface to draw on. Her figures came out muddled and blurry.

"Ellie Jane, what are you doing under there, for heaven's sake?"

She turned to see her mama's feet peeping out from underneath the dining room table. Mama wore red espadrilles, and her skinny legs looked tan and smooth.

"Nothing. I like it under here."

"Don't be silly, sweetie. It's a beautiful day. Now come out. I have to set the table for dinner."

One red espadrille tapped impatiently.

"Okay, maybe I'll go play the piano." She needed to brush up on "Chopsticks" anyway. She began to pack up the chalk.

"Just as long as you don't draw in permanent marker on the keys again."

Ellie rolled her eyes and watched as the red shoes tiptoed away. She finished packing and glanced at her palms. They were a mishmash of colors. She clapped, smudging the hues together, which created another voluminous cloud. She placed the pail's handle in her mouth and crawled, pretending to be a cow. She even gave a few quiet moos. Ellie reached the foyer and spotted Pickles at the foot of the stairs. He was watching, and cocked his head and sniffed. He was so fluffy, and his gray ears flopped from side to side.

"Pickles, I love you." She squeezed him and kissed the top of his wet nose. Pickles relented. He was used to her eight-year-old clutches.

"I love you, I love you, I *love* you." She squeezed him even tighter. Pickles squirmed, but her grip was pretty firm.

"You know you're torturing him. He hates you for it."

Ellie looked up to see Max. He shook his head, and his arms were folded in front of his chest. He smirked and batted his brown beady eyes. His strawberry blond hair was extra puffy today. He was the tallest boy in the seventh grade, and he took every chance to remind her of that.

"No, he doesn't. He loves me as much as I love him." Ellie squeezed Pickles again and gave him another kiss.

"Sure, he does, Smelly Ellie." Max poked her with his left foot. She could see tiny blades of grass in the treads of his Converse sneakers.

"Don't touch me." She gritted her teeth. She growled a little too.

"Look at you. Your feet are filthy, your hair is out of control, and your shirt is ripped."

Ellie wore tattered denim shorts, and her green T-shirt was torn in the lower-left corner. Her curly dark hair was tied up into two pigtails, but they must have fallen out during the under-table art project.

"Who cares? I'm not having tea with the queen." Ellie patted Pickles on top of his head. His fur was so soft, like fuzzy cotton balls.

Max squeezed past and climbed the stairs, still shaking his head.

"Where are you going?"

Ellie picked up Pickles. She cradled him like a baby doll. He stretched out his paws and dangled his head towards the floor.

"None of your business." Max continued to climb.

Ellie followed with Pickles in tow, but she couldn't catch up, since Pickles weighed a good twenty-five pounds.

"Wait for me," she hollered.

But she was too late. Max reached his bedroom door and shut it in her face. He smiled as he slammed it.

"What a meany-pants," Ellie said to Pickles. She gave him another kiss and set him down. Pickles took this as his opportunity to escape, prancing downstairs.

"What to do, what to do," Ellie whispered to herself.

Her mini table with tea service and Paddington Bear seemed unappealing, and Barbie's Dreamhouse was boring too. She had already cut off Barbie's and Skipper's hair, so what was left to do with them?

Ellie decided to spin. She spun three to four times, just enough to get a little dizzy. When she stopped, she faced her bedroom door, which looked surprisingly bare. Ellie wrinkled her nose and shook her head; she closed her eyes and then reopened them. Something was off? That door was never empty. Where was her straw hat?

Last summer Ellie went to the Topsfield Colonial Festival with Jessica Cartwright. They learned to make apple butter and decorate straw hats. The hat was no bigger than a Mandy doll's head. It was a sunny shade of yellow, and there were many things to adorn it with. Ellie chose pale pink and indigo dried flowers. She glued them to the base and finished it off with a silky green ribbon. Ellie hung this hat on her bedroom door, and it had sat there ever since.

She scanned the floor to see if it had dropped, but no hat was in sight. There was only one possible explanation to this mystery. Max had stolen it. Hats do not magically walk off bedroom doors. She marched across the hall and pounded with both fists.

"You open up this instant, mister. You hat thief," Ellie screamed. She continued to pound.

"Open up before I call the cops."

Max released the door, knocking her back.

"What's your problem? You are such a pest."

The door was only partially open, and he stood in the center, blocking it.

"Where is my hat? I know you took it," she snarled.

"What hat? What are you talking about? I don't have time for your monkey business" Max yawned.

"The hat that hangs from my bedroom door. The one I made at the Topsfield Colonial Festival. It's missing, and I know you took it." This time Ellie shook her fist.

Max extended one hand and gave her a small push.

"I didn't take your stupid hat. Now go away and leave me alone."

"I know you took it." Ellie tried to re-gain her balance by pressing her heels into the carpet.

"Prove it." And he slammed the door.

Ellie buzzed her lips and clenched her jaw. She hated him. Max was always so mean, and she just wanted to be his friend. A few weeks ago, she tried to follow him to the playground by taking the marsh shortcut. He spotted her and warned of serious danger. Quicksand was ahead and she would sink all the way up to her neck and be stuck forever. She believed him. What a fibber.

Prove it, huh. Okay, fiddlesticks she would. Ellie marched into her bedroom and rummaged in her desk for her tiny notepad and mini pencil. She opened her closet and reached on top for her Sherlock Holmes hat. She placed it on her head, grabbed her backpack, and fastened it to both shoulders. She slipped on her hot pink flips-flops and white mirrored sunglasses, and opened up the baby notebook. Ellie pressed down hard with the pencil and wrote in all caps: SUSPECT NUMBER 1: MAXWELL JAMES POTTER. She placed the tiny notebook into her top-left shirt pocket and tucked the pencil behind her ear. She made her way downstairs, taking two steps at a time, racing for the back door through the kitchen.

"Where do you think you are going, young lady?" Ellie's mom was chopping carrots on a cutting board at the center island. Her reading glasses were pulled halfway down her nose, and her blonde hair was tied up in a high ponytail.

"A crime has been committed," Ellie said midstride.

"Freeze." Her mom pointed an index finger.

Ellie stopped and glanced back, but she kept her sunglasses on. "What?"

"A crime has been committed?" Ellie's mom continued chopping.

"A prized piece of art is missing from my room, and I am having an investigation to catch the thief."

"Interesting, Harriet the Spy. Well, dinner will be ready in less than an hour, so wrap up the mystery before we eat." She pointed her finger and said, "Unfreeze." Ellie continued outside.

Yellow daffodils bordered the driveway. Ellie had an urge to pick one, but she knew she would get in big trouble, so she resisted. Her dad, Jake, was in the backyard mowing the lawn. She saw him as he made his way back and forth. He wore white shorts, an undershirt with grass stains, and boat shoes with no socks. Pilot sunglasses dangled from his ears. Three large garbage bags filled to the brim with clippings lined the back patio. Her dad shut off the motor and filled a fourth bag. She ran at full speed towards the overflowing heaps. They looked so soft and fluffy. Perfect to jump into.

"Don't even think about it, freckle face."

Ellie slowed to a light jog and stopped short.

"What's up, Doodlebug?" Ellie's dad tugged at one of the pigtails peeking out from underneath the hat.

"Looks like you are in search of a mystery," he said as he gulped down a glass of iced tea. The glass was sweaty with tiny drops of condensation.

"Well, as a matter of fact, I am having an investigation and I have a few questions for you. Please have a seat." Ellie gestured to the patio mesh chair and took out her notebook and pencil. She flipped through the pages with her thumb.

"Well, all right then. Shoot." Jake sat down and took another large gulp of tea.

"Have you seen any suspicious activity? Noticed anything missing?" Ellie tapped the tip of the pencil on the notebook but wrote nothing.

"Hmm, not in particular. What's missing?" Jake scratched his temple.

"My hat from the Topsfield Fair. I have a number-one suspect, but I'm running an investigation to prove it." Ellie paced back and forth.

"I see. And who might that be? Max?" Jake took off his sunglasses and placed them on top of his damp hair.

"He is the only possible suspect. He has the motive, the means, and um...yeah, the opportunity." Ellie thought of all the detective mumbo-jumbo she learned from Friday's late-night movie.

"Don't jump to any conclusions. Maybe it fell on the ground or Pickles took it. Maybe Helena moved it? You know she's always moving stuff around when she cleans the house."

"Unlikely. But I will take your evidence into consideration. That will be it for now." Ellie slipped the notebook back into her shirt pocket and shook her dad's hand.

"Good luck and don't be late for dinner."

Ellie skipped down the driveway. She needed an eyewitness or a search warrant. She spotted the daffodils again and shrugged. Just one was okay. She tugged hard to pull it from the roots and inhaled its sweet, buttery scent.

"Hi, Ellie Jane. What are you up to?" Mrs. Clark said.

Mrs. Clark was their next-door neighbor. She was kneeling in her vegetable garden digging in the muck. She was an older lady with grown-up children. The Clarks gave the best candy at Halloween. They always had loads of Reese's Cups, and they let you take two or three.

"I'm having a serious investigation. My hat from the Topsfield Fair was stolen. Have you seen any suspicious activity? Is anything missing from your house?" Ellie tucked the daffodil behind her ear.

"Nope, haven't seen anything out of the ordinary. I'm sorry you lost your hat." She winked.

"Hi, Max." Mrs. Clark waved with one of her gardening gloves.

Max was riding towards them on his blue ten-speed.

"Hi, Mrs. Clark. Hi, Smelly Ellie." Max screeched to a halt.

"Where do you think you are going? Dinner is soon." Ellie stuck her tongue out.

"Don't worry about it, nosey. I'll be back in half an hour." He smacked the brim of her hat and continued to peddle down the driveway.

Ellie watched until he disappeared.

"Bye, Mrs. Clark. I gotta go." Ellie waved and ran as fast as she could inside and up the stairs.

Max's room was disgusting. It smelled of ratty old gym socks. There were comic books, clothes, two bags of potato chips, and a half-eaten ham sandwich on a plate on the floor. She checked her Hello Kitty wristwatch. She probably had a good fifteen minutes to search before the suspect would return.

She opened his dresser drawers, surveying the contents, and then slammed them shut. She examined his desk, but there were only loose papers, uncompleted math homework, and a Hershey bar. Ellie hopped to the floor and crawled on her hands and knees. She gagged from the foul stench. She threw clothes and comics to the side to clear a path, and ended up on the left side of his bed. She lifted up the comforter and poked her head under. A flat notebook was next to a few copies of *Mad* magazine and an army-green sleeping bag. Ellie grabbed the notebook and opened it. There were various love notes and hearts drawn to a Candy Finkle. Ellie snickered. Max was in love. Gross. She slipped the notebook back under, stood up, and took a final scan, stamping her foot.

She knew he had to have the hat, but where was it? Ellie squinted and tried not to cry. She hated when he made her cry. She had an urge to kick the nightstand, but she didn't. This time she needed to teach him a lesson. She would get even.

Ellie had another seven minutes before he returned. She slipped out and made her way across the hall.

She needed to think of something clever. If she went too over the top, he would figure it out and then she would be dead meat. Ellie looked at her dresser. There was a large silver boom box, a pink flowered jewelry case, and a glass tray filled with perfume samples. Her mom gave her one every time she got a free gift at the Dillard's make-up counter. The bottles were various shapes and different shades of tan, yellow, and pink. Ellie stared at the lovely bottles, contemplating their beauty.

She walked over to the tray and selected six small bottles. She picked the ones she liked the least and tiptoed back to Max's room. The gym-sock smell knocked at her nostrils, but she ignored it. She placed all six bottles on top of Max's dresser. She lined them up neatly and in alphabetical order. Then one by one she opened a drawer and dumped the contents out. Ellie made sure each drawer got every last drop. There was no need to plug her nose now. She shook the perfume onto the lining of the drawers as well as the contents. She wanted the smell to stick for a long time.

She glanced at Hello Kitty and gathered up the empty bottles and ran out. She shut her door and leaned against it.

"Good Job, Ellie Jane," she said to herself, and gave a small clap.

Ellie placed the empty bottles back onto the mirrored tray. She mixed them in between the full ones, then took off the plaid Sherlock Holmes hat and threw it onto the bed.

"Ellie, dinner," her mother called.

"Okay. I'll be down in a minute."

She glanced at her reflection in the mirror and re-tied the pigtails so they were taut. She licked her forefinger with some spit and then rubbed the loose hairs to make them stick.

In the kitchen, her mom was placing the salad bowl onto the dinner table and her dad was pouring himself a glass of cranberry juice. Max was sitting down, already serving himself.

"Good evening," Ellie sang loudly.

They all turned.

"Max and Candy sitting in a tree, K-I-S-S-I-N-G..."

"You went into my room. I'm going to kill you." Max stood up and lurched forward. His face was fiery like a plump tomato.

"Cut it out. That's enough," Ellie's Dad yelled. He looked at Max and then Ellie. His hands were outstretched like he was trying to referee a boxing match. "Both of you say you're sorry."

"Sorry," Max mumbled. He sat back down and pushed food around his plate.

"Sorry," Ellie whispered, but she shook her head "no" as soon as her dad turned.

Ellie sat down and served herself a large heaping spoonful of mashed potatoes. She piled it high so it resembled the Matterhorn from Disneyland.

Max stared and plugged his nose.

"Jesus, Ellie, did you dump a whole bottle of perfume on? That smell is disgusting."

Ellie smirked and leaned in close. She motioned for him to lean in too. She looked him in the eye.

"Get used to it, 'cause pretty soon you will too."

Max shook his head and blinked as Ellie continued to stare and nod.

"Huh?" Max said.

"Yup!" she smirked

Pickles yelped loudly from the kitchen hall. Ellie stood up on her chair. The pup was lying down, stretched out vertically, chewing on a tiny straw hat clutched between his fluffy front paws.

MUTED SPLENDOR

◇◇◇◇◇◇◇◇◇◇◇◇◇◇◇◇◇◇◇◇◇◇◇◇◇◇◇◇◇◇◇◇

It was less complicated when it was silent. I got on the ground. I had to go low. The chair was too high, the light fixture blinding. Snowy haze radiated from the rafters, and I squished my eyes to clear the fuzz. When I reopened them, Faith was shouting from above. At least I thought she was. Leaning over, she blocked the bright shimmer and I couldn't read her lips. I lay on the concrete, arms and legs splayed out wide. It was cool and quiet except for my head vibrating with the foot traffic.

"Get up, you asshole," she signed. "You are so fucking embarrassing." Her signing was exaggerated and violent.

She pressed both of my aids into my left palm. I sat up and hooked them on, but contemplated leaving them off.

"Calm down," I signed back, making the same sweeping gestures.

"I don't know why you have to make a scene." She offered her hand and pulled me to my feet.

Restaurant patrons pretended to mind their own business, but I could see them point and glance. The guy in the plaid shirt kicked his girl's shins and nodded in my direction.

I had felt pretty good on the L train. Subways relax me with their rhythmic bouncing and hushed chaos. A baby's muted scream, the homeless guy shaking a cup for loose change, and the tight squeeze into a packed car. I felt sublime by the time we got to Bedford, but when we arrived at Egg, I was nauseated. The lights glared, beeps chimed, and the muffled echoes were unbearable. I got on the floor and chucked my aids. Big deal. I didn't give a fuck. It's not like this was the first time she had seen it. We're twins, except she can hear.

"Eli, let's go." Her signing was less violent now.

She slammed two twenties onto the table and apologized to the host. The carnage was minimal. Some yellow runny egg goo and breakfast potatoes were strewn below. She grabbed my elbow and dragged me out.

"We're not in high school anymore. Grow the fuck up." She rolled her eyes and put her hands on her hips. Her long dark hair blew across her face. She looked like Cousin It. I smiled.

"I know. I'm sorry. I got dizzy and panicked. Forgive me?"

"Eli, I love you, but get your shit together. I guess we can cross Egg off the list too. Their biscuits and gravy were pretty damn tasty. Oh well. Let's go."

"No, it was way too hipster. We should have stayed in Bushwick. I'll make it up to you. I promise."

Pedestrians stared as we signed. They turned their heads and whispered. It was totally obvious. It was amazing that they thought that I didn't see them, or maybe they just didn't care.

"Take a picture. It will last longer," Faith yelled and signed to me.

Faith is the best. I don't know what I would do without her. She is seven minutes older, but at times it felt like seven years. She yanked her hair out of her face. No more Cousin It. It wasn't too cool out despite the wind. It smelled of daffodils even though it was only the first week in March. Punxsutawney Phil had predicted that spring would come early, but that lying rodent was usually wrong. Maybe this year he didn't see his shadow?

"Eli, look at me." Faith's fingers were in my face. Her nails were chewed down to the raw, rosy cuticles.

"I have to take the train into the city to get to my poly sci class. It's going to take a bit to get to Washington Square. Are you okay? Maybe you should try and make an appointment with Dr. Silverstein?"

"I'm fine. I don't need to talk to the shrink."

"That's debatable. Keep your hearing aids on and go straight home. Especially since Howie is not with you."

Howie is my dog. He helps me when Faith is not around.

"Text me when you get to Bushwick."

Faith waved and walked down Third Street, suede fringe jacket swinging as she sauntered. Her steps quick and dancer-like. People never thought we were related, let alone twins. Faith is petite, with long willowy limbs and porcelain skin. I'm six foot two with blond hair and an olive complexion. We are polar opposites and yet so connected. I forgave her for her awful taste in music—Katy Perry, what a joke.

It was quite sunny, and I didn't feel like going back to Bushwick. It would be a shame to waste the day. I decided to go to McCarren Park and read my book. I was rereading *A Prayer for Owen Meany*. John Irving was one of my favorite authors. I wrote stories and was going to study creative writing at Gallaudet University, but it was too far from Faith, and I had never been to school with people who couldn't hear just like me. Might have been weird or maybe it would have been fantastic. Anyway, doesn't matter now.

I liked when the sun beat down on my face. The rays of sunshine penetrated my skin and traveled down my esophagus. I gulped it down in thick gobs. A pewter-tinted French bulldog panted and yelped on the corner. I love a barkless bark, a rainbow of yawns. I wasn't paying attention and got whacked into the entryway of Mast Brothers chocolate store. Pressed up against the chilly glass, I felt the doorjamb dig into my left hip. Some rotund, hairy UPS guy was yelling at me. His mouth gaped, tongue speckled with white dots. He smelled of onions. I didn't have my aids on, and I didn't need them to guess what he was hollering.

"What the fuck, asshole, are you deaf? Pay attention!"

I yelled back, but just bleeps and honks. I marched towards him, signing. He shuffled backwards and put his hands up like he was surrendering. I could read his lips now.

"Sorry, sir. I didn't know." He bowed his head, and the chestnut-shaded cap tumbled onto the pavement.

I gave him the finger and turned towards McCarren. I dug deep into my back denim pocket, fishing for the Vicodins I stored that morning. I jerked them out, dusted off the lint, and swallowed both with one swig of Smartwater. Hopefully, these wouldn't have the same effect as the ones from the L train. I turned one hearing aid on. I was in the mood only for ambient clatter, just enough to get by. I didn't need another delivery guy to mow me down.

My vision was extra clear today. I could see colors in vibrant 3D, and my sense of smell was off the charts. Maybe I had gotten a special dose of those to make up for losing one? I spotted Earwax Records and went in to browse the album covers. It was my favorite store. They have an earlobe logo, which pretty much sums me up. I headed over to the jazz section and flipped through the Cs. I was in desperate need of *John Coltrane—Blue Train and Impressions*. Milk crates of albums lined my room, filed by color and genre. Earwax had a constant steady bass. It pulsated from my fingertips to my toes.

A pretty girl flipped through the Es. Butterscotch hair piled into a messy mound. She wore an army fatigue jacket and thick tortoiseshell spectacles. I could see her flip an LP and then glance. She probably spotted the aids and wondered why a deaf guy was in a record store. I looked down but could feel her gaze as I ran my palm along the smooth plastic. She smiled. It was a crooked crescent moon. I turned to see if it was for someone else, but nobody was behind me. She waved twice with her index finger. I was still pretty fucked up from the Vicodin and seeing double. I tugged a lock of hair, indicating the aids. That would do it; it always did.

She shifted her gaze down. It's sad how predictable people are; not that there aren't kind and thoughtful folks, but this was New York City. She rifled through her satchel and pulled out tissues, a tube of lipstick, and Tic Tacs and then tossed them back. Her bag was stuffed to the brim, gray hoodie spilling out. They had to have those John Coltrane LPs, but it looked like they just had three copies of *My Favorite Things*, which I already had. It was time to get back to the original plan, which was to read in the park. I needed to make the best of my time, since I'd skipped three classes. Faith would kill me when she remembered. I flipped the LPs, and they fanned into a reclining slump. I turned and she was right in front of me. She smiled her crooked crescent moon and smelled of white jasmine and mint. She handed me a hot-pink Post-it Her handwriting was neat and bubbly.

Hi! My name is Casey. I love John Coltrane too. What's your name? :)
She outstretched her hand and gave me the stack of pink Post-its and a pen. Her nail polish matched the paper perfectly.

Eli, I scribbled.

"Hi, Eli," I read on her lips.

I mouthed "hi" back and shrugged. I mean, were we going to have a conversation on hot-pink Post-its? It was ridiculous. I motioned to my watch and scooted in between the rows. Wisps of butterscotch tresses loosely escaped the back of her bun. I hurried out and turned on the other aid. It was almost rush hour, and I needed to be alert. I squinted at Earwax and watched her wave through the front window. Her hand skimmed just below the white neon earlobe.

– ✺ –

When I got back to Bushwick it was almost a quarter past five. Howie wagged his tail, and I got on to the parquet to hug him. He had this thing about licking the back of my neck. His tongue was scratchy and he stunk of Milk-Bones, but it was pure love. Mom was in the kitchen sipping a cup of chamomile tea and reading *The New York Times*. She set the pages down on the counter.

"Hi, honey. How was your day?"

Or that was the gist of it. She never really got the hang of signing, but she tried. My dad made the whole family take classes when we were three. Faith, of course, picked it up best.

"Okay, I'm going to do my homework."

She nodded and went back to reading. She was engrossed in the lifestyle section. She loved to peruse the engagement announcements. Howie trailed and I abandoned my backpack on the carpet. I crashed onto the bed and kicked off my Chucks. That Casey girl was funny. I never had much luck with girls. How would we communicate? I didn't know any deaf girls, or guys for that matter. My parents were of the mindset of mainstreaming. The real world was full of people who could hear, my pops said. Might as well get used to it. My high school assigned me an ASL interpreter named Juan, who was pretty much the only friend I had in high school besides Faith.

The switchblade in my pants pocket burrowed into my quad, so I pulled it out and plopped it onto the nightstand. I was a resident of New York City and deaf; I needed to be prepared.

I wondered what it would have been like to go to a school with people who were just like me. The closest I got was a deaf theater club my mom enrolled me in the sixth grade. It was cool, but I'm not much of a thespian. Most of the other kids knew each other and went to private deaf academies.

The Vicodin wore off and I contemplated taking another two, but that would make it a total of six. I rifled through the nightstand for the bottle, popped off the cap, and counted four. I needed to cool it. Matt from my American lit class got them from his dad, who was a cardiologist at New York Presbyterian, but he was in Cancun for early spring break. I rolled the bottle to the rear and shut the drawer.

I put my aids next to the switchblade and got comfy, but as soon as I blinked, there was sharp drumming on my shoulder.

"What?" I signed.

It was Faith, backpack still strapped on, coat zipped up tight. Howie was next to her licking her sneakers. She smelled of the subway, steamy and desperate.

"I thought you were going to text me when you got back to Bushwick?"

"Crap. I forgot. Sorry. The day just got away from me." I sat up.

Faith ditched her bag and unzipped her coat. She paced back and forth and then skimmed her forearm along the surface of my nightstand, sweeping the entire contents onto the carpet. The lampshade crumpled, my aids flew skyward, and the switchblade leapt to the foot of the bed. Howie jumped.

"Jesus," I signed.

"Fuck, Eli. It never ends with you. I know that you skipped three classes today. It's Tuesday, not Wednesday."

"What? Oh shoot. I thought it was Wednesday, for real." I squinted; it was hard to see, since she had dumped the lamp on its side and shattered the bulb.

"Cut the shit."

Her face was crimson and bloated.

"I don't understand why you are so upset." I tried to hug her, but she shoved me into the ridges of the closet. The planks dug into my spine in linear spasms.

"I'm done, Eli. I'm not cleaning up your messes anymore. You are twenty. I'm sorry that you can't hear and that you got meningitis and I didn't, but that was eighteen years ago. You don't want my help or anyone else's. You just want to bury your head in the sand, lie, and fuck with the rest of us."

"Faith, calm down. So, I skipped a few classes. What's the big deal?"

"Oh, and don't think I don't know about the Vicodin. We can't go to half the restaurants in Brooklyn because of your medicated freak-outs."

It was only handful, maybe three?

"Faith, sit down. Can I get you some water?" Her chest expanded into a wide accordion. I moved closer, but she swatted at me like I was a pesky mosquito. She picked up my Chucks, a textbook, an iPod, and hurled them. Tears surged and her face was moist. She started signing the names of all the restaurants that had banned us. How she had missed her senior prom because of my allergic reaction to penicillin, and how she declined Princeton for me. "For what? You don't even go to class, for fuck's sake."

"Done! I'm moving in with Pete. Mom and Dad already know. Life is short, Eli. Stop wasting yours."

She wiped the snot from underneath her nose, snatched up her backpack, and sprinted out.

I stood in the middle of my room, mouth ajar. Howie had no idea what to think either. He glanced at the door and then at me, pacing and panting. She totally went ballistic. Maybe she needed a few days to calm down and hang with her man, or maybe she was stressed about midterms? What did she care if I popped a few pills and skipped a class or two? I still got straight As.

–⚙–

Three weeks passed since Faith and I had that epic fight. I tried to text her, but she ghosted me. I went to Pete's a bunch, except he said that she was in class. At least that's what he tried to sign through the front-door crack, gold chain hooked and dangling loosely.

I missed her. I missed her tiny hiccup chuckle, her stinky patchouli incense, and how her left eyebrow twitched. It was like one of my arms had been ripped from its socket. I wandered the city, a deaf armless zombie. I went to McCarren and skipped class. But that wasn't new. Howie came with me. He had to since Faith had frozen me out. I finished *A Prayer for Owen Meany* and started *Rabbit Run*. Spring was in full bloom. The tulips were intoxicating, and the miniature pre-k soccer brigade stumbled on the field like drunk old men. I didn't know how to fix this; we had never gone this long without communicating. She was my best friend. She was my ears.

I inhaled the sharp familiar scent of jasmine. I looked up and there she was. It was the Earwax chick, the one with the pink Post-its. Her hair was down in loose curls, but she still smiled that crooked crescent moon.

"Hi, Eli. How are you?" she signed.

I shot up, pressing my spine into the cool planks.

"I know a few signs," she continued. "I'm just learning. I take it as part of my psychology curriculum at NYU."

She sat down, and the slats quivered. She dipped her hand into her purse, pulling out a Five Star notebook. Her nail polish was a robin's egg blue. Come to think of it, so were her eyes.

I WISH I KNEW MORE, she scribbled. I LOOKED FOR YOU AT EARWAX.

She handed me the notebook.

MOSTLY BEEN COMING HERE AND READING. HAVEN'T BEEN IN THE MOOD FOR THE BASS. IT MAKES MY ANKLES QUAKE.

YEAH, IT'S PRETTY HEAVY. I SAW YOU THERE A FEW MONTHS BACK WITH A GIRL, THE ONE WITH THE DARK HAIR; SHE SIGNS TOO. IS THAT YOUR GIRLFRIEND?

She passed the notebook back.

NO, THAT'S MY SISTER. WE ARE TWINS.

She flashed her crescent moon; it was lovely in a goofy sort of way.

We filled up fifteen pages. It was just small talk and silly questions, but then it felt like more. The print of her curlicue script was calming, and after an hour or so it didn't seem strange to pass the bound paper back and forth. It was a record of our story etched in messy doodles and aimless scratches.

"I liked you the second I laid eyes on you. I don't know why," she signed.

We met at McCarren almost every day and texted too.

WHAT'S IT LIKE TO NOT HEAR?

No one had ever asked me that. I couldn't remember what sound felt like. I'd been deaf since I was two. There is a calm beauty in the endless silence, being on the periphery watching in slow motion. The details don't get past me. A handshake or a hug, the bounce and silent yells of a pickup basketball game, the constant thump at Earwax.

BUT DON'T YOU LONG TO HEAR?

NO. I ENJOY THE SILENCE. I DON'T KNOW ANY DIFFERENT.

It seemed okay to see it embossed in ink.

IT'S BETTER TO BLEND IN. IMMERSE MYSELF.

BUT WHAT ABOUT YOUR COMMUNITY? AREN'T YOU CURIOUS ABOUT THEM?

I hadn't thought about that in a while, but the idea began to gnaw at me like icicles thawing in the blistering sunshine. Drip, drip. Who was I? A deaf guy with no deaf friends? That was pretty fucked up.

YOU SHOULD MAKE UP WITH FAITH.

I knew that, but Faith wanted nothing to do with me. That fight made my stomach shrink, and I was still that armless zombie. I wanted things to be like they were. To tell her I was a selfish dick and that I took her for granted, but the words were buried so far down that they reached the edge of my toenails.

SHE WOULDN'T UNDERSTAND.

YOU DON'T KNOW THAT, Casey wrote.

This was the deck of cards I was dealt, and I had to adapt. Sure, it was harsh, but it was true. My dad was right; it was a hearing world, and Faith was a part of it. She didn't know what it was like to be me, and I guess I didn't know what it was like to be her.

Casey entwined her pinkie with mine so our fingers were linked into one chubby digit. The mini soccer brigade continued with their tiny kicks and wild celebrations, jumping and spinning in unapologetic delight. Their happiness was contagious.

THINK ABOUT IT.

I nodded, but Faith wasn't ready for me. Not by a long shot. Maybe I wasn't ready for her either?

The Vicodin didn't call to me anymore. I wanted to feel. To soak in Casey's weirdness and sunny glow like it was vitamin D. I ordered the Gallaudet course catalog. It couldn't hurt to take a look, right? Casey's skin was soft and plump, and she kissed me just below my aid. She had loads of friends, waved and said hi to everyone on the street. She was definitely not a New Yorker. We were a lopsided bumbling heap, but somehow we made sense that summer. I wrote Faith a letter in August. I sent it registered mail. But no reply, at least not yet.

–⚙–

It was the start of the school year, just after Labor Day, hot and sticky. The city was ripe with the stink of warm garbage and pepperoni pizza. I was kind of going to miss it even though it made me gag. It smelled like home, a mishmash of delicious and disgusting.

I sat in the Delta Sky Lounge at LaGuardia.

"Are you nervous?" Casey signed. She took my hand and squeezed it.

"A little. But it feels good."

"Promise to email."

"Of course, babe."

She leaned into the crook of my shoulder. I was going to miss that.

I closed my eyes to watermark her scent into my memory. We wouldn't be the same when I returned, but that was okay.

I blinked.

"Flight is boarding in fifteen minutes."

I nodded and twisted around.

Faith stood in front of me; Pete, ten paces behind. Her dark hair was matted and tangled in long chunks; she twisted her fingers together nervously. She sniffed.

"Hi, Eli, long time no see," she signed.

I waved from my seat. I wanted to leap up and throw my arms around her and hug her tight until it didn't matter, till my missing arm was fused back in place. But she was fragile like a gazelle, so I stayed glued to the leather bench.

"C'mon, Pete, let's get a cup of coffee," I read on Casey's lips.

She motioned for him to follow, and they linked arms and headed into the Dunkin' Donuts at gate A52. Faith sat down and left one seat in between us.

"So, you're finally doing it."

"Yup, it was time."

"I'm proud of you, Eli. Gallaudet will be good for you."

"You think?"

"Absolutely."

"How are you? Did you get my letter?"

She nodded.

"I miss you," I signed.

She was biting her thumbnail, and I could see her cuticles were still chewed down to the raw, rosy bits. She was skinnier than I remembered.

"Faith, I'm sorry, I never meant..."

She waved me off and eyed the blue carpet for a few minutes before getting up. Her eyebrow twitched.

"Well, I just wanted to say goodbye and wish you luck. Break a leg and all that."

I stood and towered over her. I took one step but then stopped short.

"I love you, Faith."

She stared, eyes watery and bloodshot. She sniffed and dabbed her nose. She nodded and patted my bicep twice.

She spun and signaled to Pete that she was coming, peering at me one last time. She sort of halfway smiled and then strolled back down the terminal towards baggage claim. She got smaller and smaller until she was just a tiny dot sashaying with her wild hair. And then she was gone.

–⌖–

Gallaudet is green. Green with thick brick structures and a blue sky littered with puffy cotton balls. My aids are off. I don't need them here. Everyone signs like we are a giant symphony, nuanced and perfect. It's graceful and booming. It's calm compared to Bushwick. I find the silence eerily robust and yet lovely. It's like some kind of muted splendor, and for the first time I feel like I can finally hear.

THE RELUCTANT SPECTATOR

◇◇◇◇◇◇◇◇◇◇◇◇◇◇◇◇◇◇◇◇◇◇◇◇◇◇◇◇◇◇◇◇◇◇◇◇◇◇

Hot, wet tears streamed down Emily's face. She attempted to wipe them away with her sleeve, but a potent blast of wind fought her balance on the bike. She continued to peddle along the path, scuttling over tiny rocks and pieces of driftwood. The sun peeped out from the marshmallow clouds and heated up the back of her neck. Emily thought she tasted the salty sea air, but it was just those pesky tears. Neither the sound of music from her iPod nor the rhythmic peddling could distract them away. She breathed in and then exhaled in an effort to bite them back, and turned onto the pebbled driveway. The bike bumped and trudged its way through.

The rented cottage was a ramshackle Cape Cod gray with forest-green shutters and flower boxes in each window. Red geraniums cheerily poked their way out. Emily hopped off the bike and pushed it like she was Sisyphus. She stopped at the first flower box and glanced at her pitiful reflection in the large windowpane. She studied the red petals for a second before pulling a few off and crumpling them. They left a trail of wrinkled red dots in her wake. What was the matter with her, for Christ's sake? Today was her birthday, her thirty-fifth birthday.

Thirty-five, single, and on vacation with her dad. It was pretty pathetic; at least that's what she kept telling herself. She plopped down on the grass and surrendered into the muffled raspy sniffs. She felt fifteen, not thirty-five.

Emily never got upset about her age or her single-girl status, and loathed the type of women who whined about it. She didn't hang with bobbleheads whose sole focus was to wrangle a husband. She was more than just whom she was with. She was herself and that was good enough. But something had happened today. It was like she had woken up from a long winter's hibernation. A giant grandfather clock chased her with its hands winding their way round and round. She blinked and ten years had whizzed on by. All her friends were married with kids, and where was she? Why didn't she pay attention? How was she still standing in the same place glimpsing life in the rearview mirror?

"Do you have a boyfriend?" family friends always asked.

"No."

"Well, why not? You are pretty adorable."

It felt like an accusation. Like there was a reason behind her solitude, like something was wrong with her and it was buried down deep below her kidneys. She felt like a defective robot that needed to be sent back to the factory.

Anyway, she didn't feel adorable all the time. Los Angeles was full of adorable women. Pretty girls were the norm, so why would anybody notice her? She wasn't a size two, tan, or blonde. In fact, she looked like a very pale vampire. "You're just like Carrie Bradshaw," her mother said, but Carrie had way more dates and clearly a better wardrobe.

Emily scowled, grunted, and tried to mop up one more time, but it was no use. She was a certifiable mess. She lay flat on the grass with her arms and legs splayed out wide. It looked like she was about to do snow angels on the perfectly manicured lawn. She gazed at the sapphire sky and tried to concentrate on the puffy clouds. Her rib cage heaved up and down as she attempted to regain control of her breath. What the fuck? It's not like turning thirty-five was a surprise. It comes right after thirty-four. It's a simple numerical sequence. She attempted to control her messy, dark hair, but the bike ride had made it unmanageable. Emily stood, whirled, and marched up to the back door, pulling on the screen. She tried to not be too noisy, but the rickety old door wouldn't cooperate.

The dogs barked and sprinted to greet her. They slid across the smooth wood and bumped into one another. The big ones, Fred and Ginger, toppled her with their excitement, and little Bo licked her ankles. His tongue was scratchy. She tried to untangle from the gaggle, but Fred and Ginger were monstrous and cornered her. Their black-and-white fur was lush and soft, but they drooled constantly. She watched as a large drip of salvia hung from Ginger's thin lips. Bo, the Napoleon of the gang, stared at her in satisfaction. He knew he had spoiled her plans for a quiet entrance. She could almost see him giggle.

"Get off me, guys. Shhhh."

She pet each one to calm them down. She smiled and whispered in a soothing tone, but they barked louder and cornered her, making a great deal of commotion.

"Emily, is that you?"

Emily glared, but they continued to leap with joy and excitement. Bo's endless licking tickled, and she let out a small chuckle.

"*Happy birthday!!!*" her dad yelled from above.

He began to sing as he peered over the railing. She was waiting for the "You look like a monkey and you smell like one too" part, but he refrained.

"Where did you go?"

"Just for a little bike ride." She was still trying to untangle herself from the trio of mutts. It was an obstacle course of furry legs and tails. Every time she managed to free a limb, they switched positions. They puffed their hot, smelly breath onto her shins.

"It's a beautiful day for that!"

"Yeah," she mumbled.

He was trying to be sweet, but he was starting to annoy her. She wasn't in the mood to celebrate. Couldn't they just forget about it? She wanted to get into bed and yank the covers over her head. She would pull the shades down tight and then cry herself to sleep in peace and dignity.

He bounded down the stairs two at a time. His thick, gray Phil Donahue hair bounced with each step.

"C'mon, sweeties, leave the birthday girl alone!" His tone was a little like baby talk. He whistled and motioned. The dogs turned but then went back to smashing her again. She was sweating.

A thick knot ballooned in the back of her throat, and the tears welled up. She counted to ten slowly. *Don't be a sniveling idiot.*

"What does the birthday girl want to do today?"

"Um, not sure."

She was irritated by his happy-go-lucky attitude. This was not a day for that. He grinned and wiggled his palms like he was doing "jazz hands." She tried to force a weak smile, but it came out mangled and scary. She probably looked like a clown.

No tears, no tears, she repeated to herself. She shut her eyes and took a few *oms.*

"Do you want to go to lunch? Do you want to go to the beach? How about let's go for a boat ride?"

He counted out the options on his fingers and gave a few skips. She just couldn't muster the energy to go along. She was feeling selfish and wanted to flounder in her hollow abyss.

"I gotta take a shower."

She edged past him, avoiding eye contact. The dogs yelped and she shut the bedroom door. The jamb stuck, so she pushed on it with her hip to plug up the last inch. She leaned against it, pressing her spine into the center. She totally just blew him off, but if she had spent one more minute, she would have lost it. It was better that he not know that she was upset. She didn't want to drag him into the Bermuda Triangle of discontent. A lone tear crept out and trekked down her cheek like a drop of honey trying to escape a teaspoon. She wiped it away violently. The door rumbled like a tiny earthquake. She could feel each tremor as it slunk up her vertebra.

"Come upstairs when you are done getting ready, and we will all go to lunch."

"Okay. Thanks, Dad. Sounds great," she creaked.

She saw the shadow of his feet underneath the door crack. He was wearing tan boat shoes with black ankle socks. He didn't move an inch. He was trying to listen, so she held her breath. The loss of oxygen pushed the blood up her esophagus and puffed her cheeks into two colossal plums. The air crawled and knocked on her lips until she heard him shuffle away. His Top-Siders skated along the pine. He squeaked upstairs, pausing on each step before climbing to the next. There was a noisy pitter-patter commotion as the dogs followed. Emily gasped and regained her breath as the blood rushed back down to her ankles. She sunk to the floor, glaring at the alarm clock on the nightstand. Happy fuckin' birthday.

PUTRID PETRIE'S FUNERAL

◇◇◇◇◇◇◇◇◇◇◇◇◇◇◇◇◇◇◇◇◇◇◇◇◇◇◇◇◇◇◇◇

My mom said it was the right thing to do, to go to Mr. Petrie's funeral. The whole school would be there, and the Somerville fire chief was going to play the bagpipes. He would even wear a bright green tartan kilt. It would be beautiful. Lots of pomp and circumstance.

"Be the bigger person, Jeremy," she said as she licked her index and middle fingers and pressed down on my cowlick.

"You look very handsome."

But I didn't want to be the bigger person. I wanted to stay at home and play Super Mario Bros. What a waste of a perfectly good Saturday. I had to wear a navy blue sport jacket and a red pinstriped bow tie. It felt like a straitjacket.

"Stop fidgeting, young man. Sit still."

The chapel was pretty full. People were packed into the pews like sardines. If you weren't wearing slacks, your thighs stuck to the slippery tan wood and made that funny farting sound. It stank like sardines too. It was muggy and humid. The A/C was on the fritz, quieting its usual loud clanking, and the stench of BO floated about. The stink reminded me of Camembert. I hate Camembert. My mom dotted at her forehead with a lace hanky. Her ankles were crossed, and I could see beads of sweat travel down her calves and disappear into her purple pumps.

"J-man, J-man."

I craned my head to see Henry in the pew behind. Looked like his mom made him come too. He wasn't wearing a jacket, and his necktie was loose and askew. Headmaster Taylor would have said that he looked like a slob. He kind of did, but he probably wasn't sweating like a pig.

"Can you believe it? Putrid Petrie finally kicked the bucket," he whispered, and clapped me on the back. I laughed but then cupped my hand over my mouth.

"Jeremy, Henry, have some respect." Mom scowled and gripped the back of my neck, forcing me to face forward. It was a sea of sweaty heads. Some ladies were wearing Easter hats, big brims, straw, with oversized pink plastic flowers. They were fanning themselves with the thin manila program. A black-and-white photograph of Mr. Petrie waved back and forth.

I'm probably going to hell. I prayed all year for Mr. Petrie to drop dead and then he did, right on the front lawn outside the dining hall. It was a week ago Thursday, and I was enjoying my favorite lunch: chicken patties, rice, and apple Brown Betty. Everyone rushed out except Allyson, Henry, and me. We watched from the window, noses pressed up against the glass. A large crowd encircled him. The ambulance's muffled siren from County Line was getting closer. He wasn't moving an inch.

"Uh-oh, Bad News Bears." Allyson twirled a lock of hair, and Henry widened his eyes through his wire-rimmed glasses.

"Wow. It really worked, J-man, sheesh."

"You can't mess with that kind of stuff. It's serious business," Allyson said. She continued to twirl.

"It's just a coincidence." My fingers curled around the window's frame, and I pressed my face into the cool glass. How was this even possible? I never thought it would actually work.

He had it out for me. I almost flunked freshman geometry because of him. I didn't care that he'd taught at Abrams Academy for thirty-five years and had tenure. I could picture him scratching his white beard, decked out in a red polka dot shirt and zigzag tie. He never matched and always smelled of garlic.

"If you can't master a class as simple as freshman geometry, you might as well go fill out the Burger King application. I expect more from a starting JV lacrosse player."

I clenched my fists so tight that the knuckles turned to a creamy shade of vanilla. I mean, seriously, how important are two sides of an isosceles triangle anyway? The bagpipes blasted out a note, although it sounded flat. The fire chief was wearing his tartan green kilt, and he had a black furry hat to match. It looked like those tall ones the guards outside of Buckingham Palace strap to the bottom of their chin. He marched down the aisle, taking one gigantic step and then pausing. He blew so hard that I thought his eyes might pop out of his head. It was only one quack and then a pretty smooth "Amazing Grace." He wasn't half bad on the pipes. Where was the rest of the fire department? They could get only one stinking guy? Except it was the chief, so I guess that was kind of a big deal. I couldn't believe that this was actually happening.

The chapel's gold pipe organ joined in, and my mom yanked me to standing. I wasn't paying attention, flipping through the hymnal, and now the entire sweaty congregation was on its feet facing the center aisle. Mrs. Owen, the middle school music teacher, banged away on the keys in the balcony. Her black hair looked like Darth Vader's helmet, and her hands rumbled up and down like a marionette. My belly churned, and bile trickled up to my teeth. I wondered if they would figure it out, that this was entirely my fault.

The coffin was a rich shade of mahogany with silver bars lining the sides. Six pallbearers hauled it down the aisle. Mr. C from biology, Headmaster Taylor, Mr. Leamon from AP European history, and Mr. Boyle from linguistics. I didn't know the other two guys. I didn't figure Putrid Petrie had any friends. Five out of the six pallbearers were the same age as my grandparents. Mr. C looked like he was carrying the brunt of it. His face was heated, and his black hair and beard were soaking wet. I could hear Boyle grunt as they passed our pew. He absolutely smelled like Camembert. Mr. C caught my eye and winked. Everyone loved him. He gave extra help sessions and started an outing club where they taught you to rappel and make a tent out of a sheet of clear plastic and three logs. He didn't make students cry. They continued lugging the coffin, and for a second it looked like Boyle was going to drop it. But he jerked the silver bar up and propped it onto his hip.

Petrie was always trying to bust us for not doing our homework. It's like he was the Gestapo of mathematics.

"Who can tell me the transitive property of congruence? Anyone, anyone? What's the converse of corresponding angles postulate?"

He whacked his ruler on the desk and then wrote on the chalkboard in a messy curlicue scribble. It was impossible to make any sense of it, and before you knew it he erased it and was on to the next impossible theorem.

"Time for a pop quiz, since you rascals can't complete assignments." He smirked, strutting his way around the classroom.

The coffin had finally reached the pulpit, and we were allowed to sit down. Two wreaths of white lilies flanked both sides. Ms. Berman-Lytle, the librarian; the fire chief; and Mr. Boyle sat to the left, up front. An American flag decorated the center of the coffin. It was wrinkled and draped almost to the floor. Henry was steadily tapping the back of my seat with his penny loafer.

"Esteemed collogues, students, and alumni. We gather here today to honor a great educator, friend, and loyal veteran: Christopher Alan Petrie." Headmaster Taylor gripped the wooden podium.

I glanced down so my mom couldn't see me crack a smile. Henry snickered. "*Achoo*-bullshit-*choo*."

"Shhhh." Mom elbowed me in the gut.

It really did just sound like a loud sneeze. Allyson Tadros had perfected the "bullshit" sneeze, and most grown-ups couldn't detect it. She did it all the time in Madame Beauvais's French conversation class. Allyson was at the end of the pew wearing a flowered Laura Ashley dress. It looked just like Mom's bedspread. Petrie had had it out for her too. She got mostly As and was one of the smartest kids in the freshman class, but Petrie graded on a curve, which took her GPA down to a B+.

"Christopher Alan Petrie taught at Abrams Academy for over thirty-five years. He had some of your parents as students, led the debate team to the state championships a record eleven times, and took his craft very seriously."

The silver microphone had a bit of an echo and whistled as Headmaster Taylor paused. I mean, was anyone buying this garbage? None of the teachers liked him either. Well, except Ms. Berman-Lytle, the librarian. They were an item. Gross. Apparently, he never volunteered for study hall monitor and left the teachers' lounge a mess with coffee cups and dirty newspapers.

I decided I wanted Petrie to meet his maker right after Christmas. I sat in the back-left corner of the classroom, and pulled my Red Sox cap down low over my eyes, but Petrie had an alphabetical system of grilling students. You never missed a turn. It's not like I didn't do my homework. I did. Mom even got me a tutor. Mr. Goldstein from across the street helped me every Tuesday after lacrosse practice. Mrs. Goldstein made hot chocolate chip cookies, and I was allowed to take one as long as it didn't spoil my appetite. I really tried to study, but it was just a bunch of mumbo-jumbo.

"Jeremy Sylvester, pay attention. Are you sleeping back there? Take that baseball cap off and sit up. Given collinear points A, B, C, and D arranged as shown, if AB equals CD, then AC equals...?" I squinted at the chalkboard and then looked down at my spiral notebook. It looked like hieroglyphics, and Petrie was making his way to the back of the classroom, taking his steps like he was doing the Grapevine.

"Um, BD."

"Wrong." He shook his head and continued to walk, holding the geometry textbook open like it was the Holy Bible.

"If three sides of one triangle are equal in measure to the corresponding sides of an angle of another triangle, the triangles are...?" He was standing right in front of me; my left hand was shaking, and my number-two pencil rolled off the desk. Below, I could hear the marching band's muffled practice. They were playing the theme from *Peanuts*. Everyone was staring at me.

"Um, um...ninety degrees?"

"Wrong!"

I felt his hot breath in my right ear; the garlic stench was unbearable.

"If the hypotenuse and a leg of a right triangle are congruent to the hypotenuse and a leg of another right triangle, then the triangles are...?" My asthma acted up. I tried to take deep breaths, and pulled my inhaler out of my pocket and took two puffs.

"I, I...don't...know."

I would never be able to live this down at lacrosse. "That's what I thought. You are better than this, Jeremy Sylvester. Apply yourself. You can do this." He snapped the textbook shut and walked back to the front of the classroom.

The fire chief and his black furry hat were at the podium telling some story about how Petrie had worked central dispatch for the department. It was the weekend graveyard shift for five long years, and they couldn't have survived without him. I tried to transfer to Mrs. Cade's geometry class, but they said it was too late in the year. I faked sick, skipped class; my mom had a parent-teacher conference with Headmaster Taylor, but it never got any better. That's when I decided to take matters into my own hands. I imagined every night that something would happen to Putrid Petrie. That he would get hit by a speeding Lamborghini, get poisoned by Mrs. Hass's Taco Tuesdays, trip over a lacrosse stick, and get stabbed in the eye like a bloody Cyclops. I know it's terrible. I told you I was going to hell. I even got a book from the library on Louisiana voodoo. Allyson, Henry, and I made a burlap cotton doll and stuffed so many needles into its tummy that it looked like a pincushion. We attached a black-and-white photo of Petrie from the yearbook to its head and added a few cloves of garlic to the interior. We sewed on red geranium petals as an offering to the spirits along with a few spritzes of Mom's Chanel

No. 5. We had a tiny ceremony in my backyard by the old tire swing. We held hands, chanted, spit on the doll, and burned last winter's geometry final. Hey, I know it sounds crazy, but we were desperate. It was just a bit of silly fun, a way to let out our frustrations. We didn't really want him dead. At least I didn't.

I thought I might throw up right there on the chapel's floor. Ms. Berman-Lytle was so close to the podium's mic that she almost kissed the metal. She was clutching a crinkled-up tissue. Her eyes were bloodshot and puffy. It was still hot and you could hear the quiet hum of those manila programs waving back and forth. I tugged at my collar to try to loosen the bow tie noose. I didn't know how much longer I could take this. I gulped in more air, but it tasted like a mouthful of Saltines. My mom had a crooked half smile and draped her arm around my shoulder. Like it wasn't hot enough.

"It's okay to be sad, Jeremy," she whispered.

Was I sad? I didn't know what to think. He couldn't have been all evil. There must have been some good? Mom said everyone had it buried underneath all the muck and knotty tree branches. You just had to dig a little deeper.

"I'd like to thank you all for coming today to honor the memory of Mr. Petrie. He would have been tickled pink that you came to remember him. He wasn't the most warm and fuzzy guy. We all know that." Ms. Berman-Lytle dabbed with her crumpled tissue. Her mascara smudged, giving her two black semi-circles.

"But he was devoted to this school, and he cared for all of you. He believed in tough love, because he knew that you are all capable of so much. He wanted to push you to your limits. His expectations for himself were twofold. He was brimming with school pride and never missed an Abrams Aardvark lacrosse game. Not even if it was raining. He was there cheering in his burgundy sweatshirt and taking snapshots with his Nikon. He taught till the bitter end because he had such passion. His heart condition did not keep him at bay. He was a fighter, just like all of you."

Petrie did take photos for the yearbook and trudged around the lacrosse field in rain boots and a fisherman's cap. He clapped and cheered, chanting "Aardvarks, Aardvarks." I was in the zone when I played; it made me feel free, and I forgot about geometry and the PSATs. I loved when the rain leaked into my helmet and mud caked up my cleats.

"Aardvarks, Aardvarks. Go, Sylvester! Go!" Petrie was at the sidelines, smiling and giving me the thumbs-up.

Ms. Berman-Lytel's gaze bore a hole into the center of my chin. I wasn't certain if she was looking at me, so I twisted around and then glanced back up front.

"Thank you for your kind words. I will treasure them always." She nodded and took her seat.

The sun was setting, and an orange-pinky glow gushed through the tracery windows. It had cooled down to only a medium hot. Two US Marine Corps officers entered and saluted the coffin, white gloves and all, before folding the flag into a perfect equilateral triangle. They bowed and presented it to Ms. Berman-Lytle. A fugitive tear escaped. Dammit, Petrie. The officers were next to one another in front of the coffin. The taller one had his left hand behind his back and a shiny brass trumpet in the right. Their pants were crisp and snowy, not a wrinkle in sight. Gold buttons and badges decorated their navy officer's coats. We all rose, and the horn sang out a bluesy "Taps." The notes were low and soothing. I could taste the salty teardrops. I took a puff from my inhaler and stared at the mahogany coffin. It was simple and shiny, and the pinky-orange light cast a glittery sheen all over it. The officers saluted again, and the fire chief began his descent back down the aisle blasting those bagpipes.

I guess it was kind of beautiful. Rest in peace, Putrid Petrie.

THE ASSISTANT

◇◇◇◇◇◇◇◇◇◇◇◇◇◇◇◇◇◇◇◇◇◇◇◇◇◇◇◇◇◇◇◇◇◇

Frank's throat burned. It was scratchy, and the taste of acid crept up to his teeth. He swallowed hard and gulped down a bottle of lukewarm water. Beads of sweat trickled down his forehead, and he wiped them away violently. He turned the ignition on of his trusty blue Honda. The car started with a quiet hum.

"Get it together, Frank," he said to himself.

He wasn't going to let a stomach ulcer ruin this opportunity. After working for two wretched years, he was finally going to pitch Marty Greenberg his movie. Granted it would be while he drove him to LAX, but at least he was getting a shot. Frank crunched down on two pink chalky Tums. He glanced in the rearview mirror and combed his hand through his damp hair.

He turned the passenger seat heater up to a medium three and double-checked that Marty's soy latte was still warm. He blew on it and it whistled. Out of the window he could see Marty walking, taking two steps at a time. He had his cellphone earpiece fastened tight and was talking loudly. Frank heard his muffled rambling through the engine's purr. Marty took a few steps and then stopped, making large gestures. The waving was exaggerated and dancelike. He looked more like a Starbucks barista than a sixty-five-year-old executive. He wore crisp Rag & Bone jeans, black Air Jordans, and a navy hoodie. His white curly hair was slicked back taut, and small gold spectacles topped the tip of his bony nose. Frank didn't get why the cheap bastard didn't just order a car service. He would surely complain about Old Blue.

Marty opened the door, almost pulling it from the hinges. He sat down and didn't even look at Frank. He clipped on his seat belt and continued to yammer. His voice was high-pitched and whiny.

"Freddy, don't take the 405; it will be a nightmare. Take La Cienega," Greenberg whispered in a curt rasp. He held his index finger up like a mini stop sign and continued with his conversation.

"Frank," Frank muttered.

Every time it was something new. Frank was surprised he even got the first letter correct.

He sat in silence and went over the pitch in his head. It needed to be perfect. He had the manuscript in the back seat with handwritten notes to himself on blue three-by-five index cards. He spent weeks memorizing them, reciting every word slowly and methodically in the bathroom mirror.

FADE IN.

EXT: CAFÉ PLA BARCELONA - NIGHT (GOTHIC DISTRICT)

We hear the clanking of glasses and the bustle of the popular tapas restaurant. Twinkle lights and candles dot the landscape. It's noisy and waiters rush about speaking Spanish.

CUT TO:

The bar. The camera slowly pans to reveal a young woman, Jessica (thirty). Her back is to us. She is wearing a long white sequined evening gown and drinking a whisky sour. She is very pretty, but as the camera gets closer we can see dirt smudges across her cheeks and a pool of dried blood at the bottom of her dress. Her fingernails are filthy. She signals the bartender.

"Camarero, uno mas."

CUT TO:

Museu Picasso. Doors ajar, broken glass, ripped paintings, and three dead bodies sprawled across the entrance.

Frank beamed. It was good. He got goosebumps just thinking about it. It was clever and it was mysterious. A definite win-win. He was ready for Marty. He'd better be, because his girlfriend was so sick of hearing it that he thought she might break up with him.

Before working for Marty, Frank had had a ton of buddies, read a novel a week (mostly John Grisham and Tom Clancy), and played in a beach volleyball league in Hermosa. He couldn't believe he'd lasted this long. Marty was such a miserable son of a bitch, but he was powerful and connected to all the right people. He had a five-year development deal with Sony Pictures. They had just finished editing three films, which were set for a summer release. George Clooney, Emma Stone, and Bradley Cooper were attached as talent. Frank just needed to bide his time a tiny bit longer, and then he wouldn't have to deal with Marty's trivial bullshit and constant abuse. For Christ's sake, he was a Harvard graduate (summa cum laude). Frank was only twenty-five but he knew that he was smarter than this Hollywood lowlife.

"Francis, what the fuck are you doing? Are you trying to kill me? Pay attention. Are you sure this latte is soy? Tastes like dairy. You can't even manage to get a decent cup of coffee." Greenberg shook his head and took a baby sip. He gripped the cup with both hands curled and interlaced like knotty branches.

"Marty, it's soy. I watched her make it myself," Frank said. They had this conversation every morning. Greenberg always accused Frank of tampering with it. He wanted to and thought about it every damn day, but refrained.

"Did you check the trades today? What number are we?" Marty took another sip and screwed his face into a yellow wrinkled raisin.

"Five," Frank replied.

"Five? Are you shitting me, Freddy? You need to call and fix this. There is no reason that *Ethology Entertainment* should be anything less than number one. I expect this fixed by the time I get back from New York." Marty reached into his leather satchel and pulled out his iPad. He checked his email, tapping the screen noisily.

Frank counted to ten. He needed to calm down. Sometimes he hated Marty so bad he wanted to punch him square in the teeth. The image of him shocked and bloody made Frank smile. He used to stay up late thinking of ways to get even. Breaking all his pencil tips, lowering his office chair from the perfect setting. Wiping mayonnaise on his dry sandwiches, pouring gritty salt in his coffee, or deflating the tires in his brand-new Mercedes-Benz. Too bad Marty's daughter beat him to the punch. He couldn't believe that his Ivy League education had led him to a mere existence of picking up dry cleaning, making dinner reservations at Ago, and running errands for Marty's monthly blonde bimbo. He should get paid extra for all the pain and suffering, but usually he just got paid with added abuse. Last month he got a full cup of coffee thrown at him. The wall in the office had a large brown stain like it was a priceless Jackson Pollock. It was a wild and chaotic java masterpiece.

The coffee was just the tip of the iceberg. Frank had to ring hotels before check-in to have the aura cleansed, and babysit bratty grandchildren. The worst was Thanksgiving two years ago. Frank had just started working for Marty and got invited over for turkey dinner. He was thrilled, since he couldn't afford a ticket home to Boston. He went to House of Pies and bought a chocolate silk and pecan. His mom's favorites, but when he arrived he was put to work unloading party furniture and setting up the table. At dinnertime, he was relegated to the kitchen to eat his plate with Maria the housekeeper.

"Francis, are you listening to me? Sometimes I feel like I talk to myself. You are so fucking incompetent. Jesus, where did you get this hunk of junk?" Old Blue sputtered and grumbled along.

"Yes, Marty. I'm listening," Frank lied as he re-adjusted his grip on the steering wheel. His hands were sticking to the leather. Frank sniffed the recycled air.

"I need you to go to Chanel and get Tiffany's handbag fixed. Also, the goddamn neighbors keep parking that camper in front of the office. Get it towed. I don't want to have to stare at that piece of shit any longer."

Marty hadn't always been a first-class asshole. In fact, he was a pretty sweet kid from Brooklyn. He got picked on in high school; short, scrawny, and into Allen Ginsberg and beatnik culture. He dressed in all black and topped his curly brown hair with a beret. He snapped his fingers and went to poetry readings. On a weekly basis, the football team kicked Marty's ass for being a "freak." One day they would be sorry. He worked his butt off and got a scholarship to NYU and made his way out west, climbing up from the mailroom at the William Morris Agency.

Marty rolled down his window and dumped the remainder of the latte out. He looked at Frank and smirked. He threw the cup on the floor and crushed it. Coffee remnants seeped into Frank's freshly shampooed car mats. Marty made another phone call.

"Hi, baby, on the way to LAX. Freddy is taking me. He promised he would take care of the handbag," Greenberg cooed.

Frank accelerated. His stomach rumbled and his mouth was parched like it was full of sand particles. He swallowed the grains and gulped down more liquid. There was no way he was going to let Marty's foul mood intimidate him from this pitch. He waited patiently as Marty continued to spew more garbage and empty sentiments to the latest chick. He used the same lines over and over. Frank had heard them a million times.

"Baby, I'll call you when I land. I gotta go. Kisses."

Frank cleared his throat.

"Are you fucking sick, Francis? You better not breathe your nasty germs on me." Greenberg covered his mouth and scooted closer to the door. He crossed his legs and cracked the window, pressing his nose up against it.

"No, Marty, I am not sick." Frank rolled his eyes. "I wanted to talk to you about my screenplay. Remember, you promised that you would let me pitch to you on the way to the airport. I'm really excited to get your thoughts. I worked very hard and think it will make a terrific film." Frank spoke calmly and smiled.

"What? Your screenplay?" Marty raised his eyebrows but didn't look up, continuing to read *The Hollywood Reporter*.

"Yeah, it's a cross between *Lost in Translation* and *Delicatessen*. I think it is something that Focus Features would pick up."

Frank felt good. He had won third prize at the Ivy Film Festival at Brown University, and he had been accepted to attend USC graduate school for film in the fall. He knew he had the talent. He just needed Marty to listen and take him seriously.

Marty glared. He pursed his purple lips and took off his glasses. He squished his eyes into tiny slits and sighed.

"Listen, Freddy. I am sure your shit art-house idea is worth it to some other crappy producer. But this is the big leagues, and I don't have time for amateur hour." Marty shook his head and put his glasses back on.

"Fucking kids," he muttered.

Frank refocused his gaze and sat in silence. He gripped the steering wheel so tightly that his knuckles turned crimson. The knots in his stomach tightened up so much that they felt like they were trying to squash his organs flat. Cars whizzed by in slow motion, and he saw colors and shapes in a rainbow of blurs. The traffic was muffled like he was underwater, tumbling and sinking in hushed silence.

Frank glanced from side to side, trying to gauge where they were. He must have made a wrong turn. It looked like they were on Jefferson, far east of Rodeo. Rundown drab apartments lined the street, and two homeless guys in seven layers of multicolored outfits rummaged in a large dumpster on the corner of Jefferson and Hillcrest. They looked like puffy marshmallows. Frank pulled the car over and turned off the ignition, resting his head on the steering wheel.

"Francis, Francis!!! What the fuck are you doing? I'm going to miss my flight."

Greenberg was screaming, pink, and spitting, but Frank couldn't hear. He looked up and Marty was hollering like a monkey. Frank laughed out loud. He couldn't help it. The hoot was maniacal, high-pitched, and hard to control. He clicked the long silver button on the door handle, locking it with a snap. He continued to laugh, throwing his head back and clutching his stomach. His abs ached like he had done a thousand sit-ups, but he didn't care.

"Freddy, I am not fucking around. Turn the goddamn car on and get me to LAX this instant!"

Marty's right fist was clenched. He had inched himself to the far edge of the seat and his left hand was wrapped around the doorknob. What a wimp.

Frank unlocked the doors and opened the driver's side. He left the door ajar and sauntered over to Greenberg, who was still yelling and waving his hands all over the place. He opened the passenger door and gazed at the pathetic hooded primate. Greenberg blinked and stopped yapping. Frank was pretty imposing when he stood up. He was tall at six-foot-two and dwarfed a tiny five-foot-six Marty. Frank grabbed Greenberg's brown leather satchel and heaved it onto the sidewalk. It skidded and hit the parking meter in front. Frank heard the iPad clank and shatter with a loud spiraling bang. He leaned in, gritting his teeth.

"Get the *fuck* out of my car."

Marty gaped, clutching his cell to his chest.

"What? What?"

"You heard me. Get the fuck out." Frank leaned back. He stood erect, resting his forearm on the door.

Marty dipped one toe out and then the other. He didn't take his eyes off Frank as he hopped onto the sidewalk like a baby bunny. He shuffled a few paces backwards. Frank slammed the door. The car wobbled back and forth, shaking like a tiny Hot Wheels.

"Hand me your cell," Frank said.

"Huh? Please?"

Frank stuck his palm out. Marty plopped down the phone. Frank then drew his arm back and hurled it. It landed close to the two homeless snowmen digging through the garbage.

Frank walked back to the driver's side; he didn't take his eyes off Marty as he made his way. He sat back down and clicked on his seat belt.

"Frank, wait! Wait! I think there has been some kind of misunderstanding."

Frank slammed the door.

"Wait, Frank!!!" Marty took one step but then froze.

Frank put the car in drive and peeled away. He watched Marty in the rearview mirror dumbfounded, like a lost puppy dog. He almost felt sorry for him. Well, almost. Frank rolled down the window and breathed in the smog. It smelled like gasoline, but it was divine. His stomach didn't ache that much anymore. He smiled and accelerated, pressing on the gas pedal. The car lurched forward. The image of Marty on the curb got smaller and smaller and then turned into a tiny dot. At least this time he got his name right.

ALICE

◇◇◇◇◇◇◇◇◇◇◇◇◇◇◇◇◇◇◇◇◇◇◇◇◇◇◇◇◇◇◇◇◇◇◇

The dull pain thumped like a kick drum. It was persistent and knocked at Alice's skull in tiny fits. She felt it from the top of her ponytail all the way to her bum. She scooted her hips to the left, nudging a pesky branch that dug deep into her thigh. She tried to wiggle her toes through her wet sneakers, but they were deeply embedded in the metal spokes. Just below her right eye she felt a damp patch. The blood was bright red, like marinara sauce. She attempted to open the other lid, cracking the scabby barrier only slightly. It looked like dusk from what she could glimpse out of her good eye. The sun was setting and had left a fiery hue on the horizon.

Alice was sprawled out flat on her back and yet tangled up in her bicycle like a spider clinging to its web. She couldn't move much, and the pain in her forehead was awful. The reeds were quite high for this time of year, and it was beginning to get cool out. Goosebumps took their shape on her forearms.

"Help," she thought she yelled, but not a single note escaped her lips. She arched her back high and puffed out her ribs, but she could barely get higher than an inch.

"Hhhellpp!"

This time she heard it. It was low and subtle, but her stutter was unmistakably distinct. Who would hear her all the way out here? She could barely emit an intelligible sound and was sure that the thick reeds hid her from sight. Her mama would be furious. She wasn't allowed to ride after 6 p.m., and it looked like she was all the way down by Flanders Landing. Another no-no, especially by herself. She usually rode with Ollie, but she couldn't spot him from this angle. It was hazy, so she lifted her head higher to get a better view, but it was no use. The throbbing pain made her cranium a dense bowling ball.

The last thing she remembered was eating a giant bowl of Cocoa Puffs before getting on the bus to go to school. She hated riding the school bus. Alice didn't have many friends. In fact, just one. Ollie. Most of the other sixth graders called her names, like "freak" and "loser," or tried to trip her as she walked to class. Her uneven limp and stutter made her an easy target. They'd had a field day last winter when she wore an eye patch for three months to correct her lazy left eye.

Sometimes Alice would lock herself in one of the bathroom stalls and cry, crunched up, sitting on top of the toilet. She hugged her knees and buried her face into her dungarees. The tears soaked through and made a large butterfly pattern. Her mother tried to talk to the principal, but it only made things worse. Classmates threw crumpled papers and rotten bananas, and left nasty surprises in her gym locker. Last week she found a dead mouse dangling from her coat hook. Alice just endured. She was pretty much used to it now and accepted it as a way of life.

"You are one special little girl," her mama told her. "This will only make you stronger. You just pay them no mind and smile your way through." She ran her delicate fingers through Alice's long blonde hair and stroked her cheek. "My sweet Alice from Wonderland."

Alice's Adventures in Wonderland had been her mother's favorite book as a child, and now it was Alice's too. She carried an old tattered copy and tucked it neatly into her backpack, which she now spotted out of the corner of her crusty eye. It was resting casually by the front wheel. She underlined her favorite passages and reread them over and over.

Alice felt liberated and relaxed on her bicycle. There, she had no limp and no stutter. It was just the wind whispering as she sped along on her shiny red Schwinn. She would shout:

"Which road do I take?" said Alice.

"Where do you want to go?" responded the Cheshire Cat.

"I don't know," Alice answered.

"Then," said the cat, "it doesn't matter."

And that was their motto. Ollie's and hers.

The words were clear in her head as she shouted them. She could remember the typeface and exact placement on the page, but she knew it was muddled chaos as each sound traveled up her throat and sailed into the universe. It didn't much matter on the bike or with Ollie. He knew exactly what she was saying.

But what had happened after she got off the bus? She remembered waving to Mr. Walsh, the bus driver. He always winked and gave out Tootsie Pops. She sat in the front seat, thighs sticking to the hot green plastic. She pulled out her copy of *Alice's Adventures in Wonderland* and began to read, like usual, but after that it was blank.

Alice twisted her fingers and dug them into the mud. It felt sticky and thick, like papier-mâché from art class. It clung to her palms in hefty chunks and stunk of rotten eggs. She scratched in further, searching for a rock or knotty root to help boost her up and out of her metal cage, but all it did was coat her hands in another layer of muck. The tears trickled out in a steady stream, and she could taste the salt and blood as each drop rolled over her splintered lips.

"Curiouser and curiouser," she whispered a good six times.

It came out with the "s" elongated and doubled, but the repetition was calming and slowed the progression of tears. She took two deep breaths and dragged her head sideways. She lifted one muddy hand and clutched the top of her thigh, and then pointed her left foot like she was wearing ballet slippers. She twisted it upright and tried to drag it through the tiny metal opening. Her sneaker caught on a loose hinge, so she kicked it. A few spokes rocketed into the navy sky, catching on the moon's glistening reflection.

Her sneaker was now ripped to shreds, but Alice didn't care. At least one foot was loose. She was now able to scoot her way to seated by pulling on the metal frame and pressing down on her free limb. She was dizzy, and her skull throbbed. She touched the back of her head; it was sticky underneath her matted hair. Her right foot remained neatly entangled.

Alice examined the back wheel. Sometimes those nasty kids messed with her beautiful bicycle. They let the air out of the tires or stole her shiny silver bell. But the tires looked plump, and the bell dangled by one lone screw. It wasn't shiny anymore, and when she rang it the *ding* quacked like a sick duck.

"Off withhh their hhheadss," she said.

Alice tried to ring it again, but the same pathetic blast echoed into the tall grass. She snatched up her backpack and squeezed it. The dirt path looked level and smooth. There were no large rocks or thorny roots. She didn't see any trees or bushes. How had she crashed? There was nothing to run into. Flanders Landing was on the way to the beach, and the terrain was fairly open except for the reeds. Alice counted to ten and let out one long, breath. Dr. Doyle had told her this would calm her down. Sometimes it helped with the stuttering, but it never cured it. Not many people ventured to Flanders Landing this time of year. It was the start of fall, and the summer tourists had headed home. Only old fishermen and high school sweethearts made their way down. She could hear the tugboats puttering, and a loud blast from the foghorn made her jump.

Was she going mad? Why was she alone? Where was Ollie? What had she been doing all day, and what had happened after she got off the yellow bus? If she could manage to free her other leg, she might be able to hobble home, but that would take hours. Her limp slowed her pace to a tortoise stroll.

The reeds rustled like the bristles of that old broom her grandma used to sweep the service porch with. Alice zipped open the front pocket of her backpack and rummaged for her flashlight. She flicked it on, moving the torch back and forth.

"Heeelp, heelp."

The reeds whistled again as her vision remained blurry. The light from the flashlight generated a misty focus over the grass, and it blended into a spectacular threading mush. Crunch. The flashlight quivered as her hands shook. A midsized scruffy mutt made his way out. He circled her and plopped down, licking her toes through the tattered sneaker. His tongue was scratchy, but it felt warm and soothing on the wounds.

"Heelp," she said again. Only the "p" escaped in one trivial wisp. The mutt looked up but then returned to his ticklish slobbering.

"Heeeeelp!" She screamed so loudly that her garbled words resonated like she was shouting from the bottom of the Grand Canyon. Alice and her grandpa had visited it last summer and taken turns shouting each other's names and listening as it boomed against the ginger rocks. She pounded her fists into the earth and coughed. The new crop of tears stung at her wounds and they fled in tributaries. They felt deep and pebbled. What was going on? How had she gotten here? Who was going to help her?

If only the White Rabbit would appear. She could escape this confusion and her ridiculous life. Things would be better in Wonderland. She would have friends and adventures and no one would tease her. She could eat a delicious slice of cake to fix her limp and obey "drink me" to smooth out the stutter.

"Oh, Mama..."

Alice squished her eyes shut and hugged her free knee snug. The scab underneath her eye flaked, and fresh blood gushed in a thick channel.

"I can't go back to yesterday, because I was a different person then. Why, sometimes I've believed as many as six impossible things before breakfast. Have I gone mad? I'm afraid so, but let me tell you something, the best people usually are. If I had a world of my own, everything would be nonsense."

Alice whispered these verses to herself over and over. She grasped her free knee a little less and rocked back and forth on the chilly terrain. It was pitch black out now. The flashlight clicked, and a loud stamp quivered into the mud. A few wet chunks dangled from the tip of her elbow. Through her closed eyes, she could feel it get even darker. She tried to seal her lids tighter and bury her head into the crux of her lap, but her curiosity got the best of her. She blinked open one eye at a time. The foggy tears and crusty debris made it difficult, but as her vision adjusted she gazed upon a pair of enormous black rubber boots. She lifted her head to get a better glimpse.

"Who in the world am I? Ah, that's the great puzzle," said Alice.

LANDLADY OF THE FLIES

<>><><><><><><><><><><><><><><><><><><><><>

The flies were wily, wedging their tiny green thoraxes through miniature holes. Pea-sized, needle-sized. They sailed by, buzzing and flapping their delicate wings. I tried not to panic, but then three hummed, and four, and then seven. I was hunting them from the kitchen to the bedroom, spraying Raid in my wake, whacking them with June's copy of *Vanity Fair*. Their bloody corpses plummeted onto the Berber carpet only to be carried away in a tissue casket. I loathed the infinite sea of casualties on my terracotta tile. I'm a pacifist and a vegan, but this was an all-out war.

I rang my landlady. "Flies are back." I emailed, texted, and called. It took her seventy-two hours to respond. Meanwhile, the body count had climbed to ninety-three. I was exhausted from battle and woozy from the Raid. I'm anti-chemical anything, but I didn't know what else to do. Whole Foods didn't sell an organic all-natural bug spray.

"Sarah, so they're back?"

She panted at my doorstep, clutching the frame and smelling of whisky. She resided above, just thirty-two steps up a steep hill. I was her only tenant, living in the guesthouse. A large-brimmed straw hat shaded her sallow, bony face. It was the kind the lawn guys wore to take care of the yard. She had dark glasses on, a ripped white button-down with a quarter-sized coffee stain, and UGGs even though it was the end of August in Los Angeles. She appeared incognito, like the Pink Panther, obvious and bumbling.

"Hi, Patricia. Yes, in full force."

I widened the door, and she heaved herself in. She slinked about, inspecting crevices and craning her head toward the ceiling, sunglasses still on. I didn't get what she was doing. She wasn't an entomologist.

"I need to use your bathroom."

She sprinted to the loo, slamming the door, leaving me to hug that toxic can of Raid.

"*Namaste*," I said to myself, and I took a few *oms*.

Things had been better when Alan and Cesar owned the property. They operated at a different pace. She was on the "I'll get around to it at some point" schedule. I can be pretty relaxed about minutia; I'm a yoga instructor. But this was too much.

"Sorry about that," she said.

"Are you feeling any better?"

"Not really. Don't get cancer; don't get MS; don't get brain damage." The straw hat wobbled on her tiny bobblehead. I didn't know what to say, so I just stared at the carpet's deep ridges.

"Anyway, I think they are coming in through the bathroom vent. I saw a few sneak out." I pointed to the square above the toilet.

"Those tricky buggers. All right, let me call Trent from Orkin, and I'll call Sammy too. Maybe he can seal it up. I'll email you with an ETA."

"Thanks. Sounds great."

Patricia snatched her keys off the kitchen table and shuffled out. I gazed from the window as she staggered up the stairs, taking her steps with focus and tempo. She was such a slowpoke. She might feel better if she took a few flow classes and detoxed. The stretching would do her a world of good.

I felt sorry for her despite her crabbiness. I worried I would have to call 911. She was only sixty-nine but acted closer to eighty-nine. Her car remained stagnant in the driveway, silver sunshade blocking the windshield. Newspapers piled high, and mail remained uncollected. She didn't have friends or visitors, just one yellow cat that patrolled the deck railing like a security guard. I felt guilty when I called to have things repaired. She wasn't well, but she was the landlady after all.

Cesar told me that Patricia was a pioneering gal who had broken the glass ceiling back in the '80s. It was hard to imagine her in a position of zest and power running a law firm when she wandered the neighborhood clutching a deflated pillow. She was frail and childlike. Gangly, hair short and loose, with patches missing in the midsection.

She rummaged through the garbage checking for scraps, keeping old tattered curtains, discarded bottles of Cheer, and empty bags of Cape Cod kettle chips. Maybe she was composting? I pictured her house awash in junk. Towering stacks of magazines, chunks of black bags plumped and encircling the sofa like "Sara Cynthia Stout, who would not take the garbage out." In the mornings, bottles of merlot and pinot noir dotted each step. The empty green glass shimmered in the sunlight.

And yet the flies kept coming. Sometimes, they would take a week's hiatus, but they always returned, teeny babies and bulky grown adults. She managed to arrange for Trent from Orkin to come, but the flies just wouldn't vacate. I could feel the toxins seep into my skin, as my enemy remained immune. It's like they were on vacation only to return after seven balmy days in Maui.

I took matters into my own hands and stood on the toilet, coating the vent in thick layers of duct tape. Layer after layer. There was no way they were going to escape on my watch. I teetered on my step stool, adding sticky strips to the rim of the crawl space using the tip of a barbecue fork to secure it. It was sloppy and crooked, but I didn't care. I needed a respite from battle.

Sarah, are you home? a text from Pat chimed.

I tried to ignore it, but I'm such a peace-loving hippie.

yup. The roll of duct tape dangled from my left wrist.

"I hate to bother you, but I don't know who else to contact. I had a cortisone shot in my ankle, and I'm having an allergic reaction. Would you mind driving me to Kaiser?"

"Sure. Let me grab my keys and I will be right up."

She was waiting at her front door, gigantic brown tote slung over her shoulder and sunglasses still on. It was 8 p.m. and pitch black out.

"Thanks so much. I hate to bother you."

"It's okay."

She clutched my elbow, limped, and scowled.

"Yowee. This is about a ten. I have a high tolerance for pain, but this is pretty bad."

It took us five minutes to get down and into my Prius. Why was I her emergency contact? We weren't friends, and she hadn't taken any of my yoga workshops. I was just her tenant living below with a bunch of asshole flies. It was totally awkward.

"I wasn't always like this," she mumbled as I turned onto Franklin. She stared into the black as headlights whizzed by in fits and bursts.

I just listened. I wasn't sure if she was looking for a conversation or wanted to vent.

"Sometimes it's not even worth it."

"Don't say that. You will feel better tomorrow. Positive thinking."

"Doubtful."

She continued to mumble and puff out air like she was taking a Lamaze class. Beads of sweat dribbled down her cheek. I tried to concentrate on Garth Trinidad on KCRW, but her wheezing was quite distracting.

"Well, here we are." I pulled into Emergency.

I had to get a wheelchair and roll her in. My car waited in the drive, hazards blinking. I wanted to drop her and bolt. Dine and dash, but I felt those pangs of guilt knocking at my tummy.

Signs were posted warning of Ebola. How you get it, how you spread it, blah, blah. Bright shades of crimson and green adorned the letters, resembling a holiday card. Patricia yammered in her wheelchair at the check-in nurse about how she had just been here this morning. Her health insurance cards splayed into a laminated rainbow.

"Is this your daughter?" the nurse asked.

"No. But she could be." Patricia beamed.

"You don't have to stay." She waved and shoved her cards back into her wallet. Her fingers quaked as she inserted each one.

"Really? Are you sure?"

"No need. I can take an Uber, and who knows how long I will be? The service sucks." She gestured around and rolled her eyes. It looked pretty empty. An elderly man was taking a nap on three chairs, and a teenaged couple bickered in the corner.

"Oh, would you mind checking on Muffin? I forgot to feed him. He must be starving. Key's under the barbecue."

"Ah. Um. Okay. Sure." At least I didn't have to wait.

"Thanks a million." She turned back towards the nurse.

"There must be someone who can take me. Really, I was just here this morning. Obamacare, my ass. This is ridiculous."

I'm allergic to cats, and Patricia's energy sucked the life out of me. I just wanted to live in peace with a fly-free existence. Two empty wine bottles and a wet newspaper rested on her bottom step. The light in the garage had burned out months ago, so I had to use my phone as a flashlight. The barbecue key was just below the grill on top of a piece of charcoal. I coughed.

Her house was not awash in junk as I had envisioned. It smelled of lavender and verbena. Pat's style was Victorian. Gold embossed mirrors, cherry-colored wood, and royal blue cushions. Or maybe that was Napoleonic? The yellow cat sprinted by in a sunny haze. Shades were drawn, and the floorboards creaked. She had quite a book collection. A wall in the living room was covered floor to ceiling. *Moby Dick*, *War and Peace*, and a number of astronomy books. *Left Turn at Orion*; *Cosmos*, by Carl Sagan; and *The Grand Design*, by Stephen Hawking. I flipped through a few. I was being nosy, but I couldn't help it. She was a feeble enigma on the outside and a nerdy academic in here. Framed blueprints of constellations hung from walls, and black-and-white photos of a young Patricia in a military uniform were strewn on the shelves. She had pictures from an African safari, a record collection to rival any deejay's, and a ginormous Celestron telescope. It was perched on top of the deck, lens pointing skyward. I was reading the back jacket of Dizzy Gillespie's *Swing Low, Sweet Cadillac* when her phone rang. I slid the album back and made my way to the kitchen to feed that yellow cat. I sneezed. The ringing continued to blare until the machine picked up (of course she had an answering machine from 1995). Pat's crackly voice repeated her number and told them to leave a message at the beep.

"Pat, are you home? Pick up. It's Florence. Hello, are you there? Okay, well I'm worried, so please call me back. Hello, hello....I guess you're not there. Bye, honey."

So, she did have friends? Who was Florence, and why didn't she call her? I reached for the cat food, which was next to a swarm of pill bottles. They lined the kitchen counter in jagged rows. I clanked kibble into a metal bowl, refilled the water dish, and headed downstairs. It was time for sleep; hopefully the flies were still trapped behind my adhesive barrier. It had been a long night, and the last thing I needed was a midnight skirmish.

I saw her the next morning sorting through the garbage. Her ankle was wrapped up in a flesh-colored bandage. One crutch was tucked neatly underneath her left armpit. She hopped from can to can, bending deep and balancing on her tippy-toes.

"Hey, Pat. Feeling better?"

She popped up. Today, she smelled of chardonnay.

"Oh, hey there. Didn't see you. Yes, much better. They gave me a bunch of Percocet, so I feel pretty great now. Thanks for taking me last night. You are a lifesaver! I have a gift for you."

She pulled a robust peach from her pants pocket. I hoped she hadn't yanked it from the garbage.

"Ah, thanks. You grow this in your garden?"

I rolled it in my palm, patting its fuzzy exterior, and spotted an oval sticker. It was probably from Ralphs.

"Peaches. Nectar of the gods."

"Uh-huh. So, you are quite the astronomy buff," I said, continuing to roll my thank-you peach and stretching my calf. I was sore from the last two vinyasas.

"Well, not anymore, but back in the day. I almost got a master's degree from Princeton, but then went to Harvard Law instead. My papa said no use in being a stargazer."

"Stargazer, that sounds lovely. There is a super moon next week. I bet you can get a fantastic view from Griffith Park."

"The last one was in 1982, and the next will be in 2033. A blood moon is rare. Haven't been able to make it up to the park in years. Poor health...you know."

"Well, I am glad you are on the mend. Maybe Sam can come by and resolve the fly situation. I taped up the vent, but he can probably seal it more securely?"

"Right. Yes, of course. I'll call him tomorrow. I'm on it."

She went back to rummaging even though I wasn't done talking. I wanted to ask who Florence was.

Pat was so depressing. A garbage collector who numbed herself with booze and pills. Her bookshelf told a different story of a cultured adventurer who lived life to the fullest. How had she spiraled so deep? Did sickness and seclusion push her over the edge? Maybe she just needed positive vibes. Something to look forward to, a reminder of days gone by. Passion was the antidote to despair.

I spent three days getting ready. I got two lawn chairs from Target, a couple of fleece blankets, some turkey sandwiches from Lemonade, a cheap pair of binoculars, and a bottle of Veuve Clicquot. It was September twenty-seventh, the day of the last blood moon until 2033, and I was going to make sure that Pat saw it.

I knocked on her door.

"Pat, it's Sarah. Are you home?"

She creaked it partway. I could see a wrinkled hazel eye and the tip of her straw brim.

"Oh, darn it. Are those flies out of control again? I meant to call Sam, but I haven't been feeling well."

"I have a surprise for you. Get your purse. We are going to see the blood moon!"

She widened the door. She was still in her PJs, and it was well after 5 p.m. She smiled. I wondered if she slept in that straw hat.

"Oh, wow. Really? That is so sweet of you. I'm still not feeling great. Maybe I should stay home?"

"C'mon, Pat. I got us lawn chairs and champagne. The next blood moon isn't for another eighteen years!"

"You are right. Give me five minutes."

It was a struggle to get her up to the park. She moved like a prehistoric tortoise. Everyone turned out for the viewing. I had a friend who volunteered at the observatory, and he hooked me up with special parking. We managed to cut through Beachwood Canyon using Waze and avoided all the looky-loo traffic on Los Feliz. The charcoal sky was cloudy with murky patches of cerulean. I hoped the smoky puffs would dissipate and give us a clear sighting. Pat was bundled up in a blanket, legs stretched out vertically. Binoculars draped around her neck. She munched on a sandwich, but took only a few bites, crumbs stuck to the rim of her top lip. She picked up the binoculars.

"If you look closely you can see the constellation Capricornus, the sea goat. It kind of looks like an arrowhead. See that sparkle up and to the left? That's Vega. It connects down to Altair and then backs up to Deneb. We would have a much better view with the Celestron. Wanna take a look?"

She handed me the binoculars. I tried to see what she was talking about, but it just looked like a cluster of twinkly dots. I nodded and handed them back.

"If you get a chance to go to Australia, be sure to check out the Southern Cross. There is a stunning view of it in Kakadu National Park. It's so clear and bright, almost like thousands of tiny candles."

"Wow. You have been to Australia?"

"Sweetie, I have been all over the world."

"Can I ask you a question? Who is Florence?"

She released the binoculars to swing loose and stared at the grass.

"Florence, huh? Haven't seen her in over twenty years. Anyway, what about you? Are you a world explorer? Are you going to be a gymnast forever?"

"Yoga teacher. I don't know. I always wanted to be an architect. I was thinking of taking some classes in the spring."

"Honey, do it. Don't waste time. Life is short, and there are no do-overs. Believe me. Oh, look, it's almost peak."

The moon was now burnt-orange, sinister and yet spectacular. Pat grinned, binoculars glued to her sockets, and she was humming.

I had done good.

"It's funny to think about how small we all are, in comparison to the expansive universe. We are just tiny specs," Pat said. "Yup, teeny, tiny pieces of dust."

She leaned back, gazed, and giggled softly.

–✦–

I hadn't seen Pat since the blood moon five days ago. Her car wasn't in the driveway. I figured the trip helped and she decided to rejoin the land of the living. It rained hard on Sunday, so I decided to sleep in. I loved to hear the pitter-patter; it reminded me of growing up in Seattle. Pink polka dot umbrellas and green Hunter boots. The drought had made the droplets dreamlike and unfamiliar. I was groggy, but someone was pounding on my door.

"Hello?"

A little old lady with white hair, in a yellow slicker, stood outside. The rain pelted at her hooded head.

"Hello, dear. Sorry to bother you so early. I'm Florence, Pat's sister. May I come in?"

"Sure."

So that's who Florence was.

She stepped inside and pulled her hood down but didn't move any further than the doormat.

"I'm afraid I have some bad news. Pat is gone."

"Gone? Like missing?"

"No, dear. She's passed away."

"What? She was fine. I was just with her a few days ago. We saw the blood moon."

"As you know, Pat was never in good health. She was bipolar and erratic. She swallowed two bottles of sleeping pills and drove herself up to Griffith Park. LAPD found her two days ago."

"Oh, my God. Pat..."

I didn't know what to say. I was quiet and started to cry. Not a hysterical cry, but slow, calm tears. Her sister just stood by the door, yellow slicker moist and nodded her head. She wasn't weepy or despondent; she seemed kind of matter-of-fact. Lethargic and defeated. The end to a battle that she had waged for a long time.

–⚙–

It's been one year since Pat passed on. Florence sold the property, and I moved to a cute little bungalow in Silver Lake. It overlooks the reservoir, and the exterior is cloaked in fuchsia bougainvillea. No flies, yet. I'm not gonna lie. When I hear one hum, I jump a bit. I started taking a few architecture classes at UCLA Extension, and I met a cute guy named Carl while I was grabbing a chai at Intelligentsia. Pat left me a few of her astronomy books, and that gigantic Celestron, and oh, that yellow cat that I am allergic to. I'm trying to figure out how to work that telescope. It's pretty complicated. I still teach yoga, but only three days a week.

I think of Pat often, especially on clear nights when the stars dazzle intensely or when there is a lunar eclipse, or Saturn is a ginger fireball. I think about how she dragged herself up to Griffith Park for one last hurrah, to become one with the universe and free. I picture her bundled and drunk, toasting the full moon, cursing at the flies, and dancing in that raggedy straw hat. She was finally a stargazer.

Here's to you, Pat.

CHAIN LINKED

◇◇◇◇◇◇◇◇◇◇◇◇◇◇◇◇◇◇◇◇◇◇◇◇◇◇◇◇◇◇◇◇◇

I turned, but no one was behind me. His nose was bleeding badly, and he held his head back so the crimson stream didn't flood his face.

"It's you."

"What?" I twirled again.

He gave me the side eye, and I wondered if it was best to just tiptoe away. He sat halfway up on the concrete, knees bent, looking from east to west. It seemed unlikely that he would leap up out of his stupor and chase me. His hair was messy, and streaks of dirt coated his forearms and calves. He might have even twisted an ankle, so it would have been more like a hobble. A bloody-nosed hobble. God, this was embarrassing. It wasn't supposed to happen like this...

The first time I saw him, his fluffy gray hair bounced as he tried to dunk. He stood out like a spare bowling pin. Twisted metal diamonds made tiny windows to the game. The metal fence smelled of oxidized steel, rotten and cool. He was wobbly and flailing, face babyish and yet rugged. Richard Gere from *Pretty Woman*, you might say. I saw him almost every day when I walked Paco around the reservoir. Paco sniffed at the parched dandelions and licked the tree bark soaked in canine urine. I stared as he sprinted up and down, fingers gripping the fence. Paco yelped with his baby woof, but "Richard Gere" never saw me.

I wanted to say hi, but the words were buried deep down in my esophagus. Each letter tried to climb its way up, but I bit them back with a large gulp. It didn't matter; he was too winded and entrenched in the game to hear. The ball beat against the concrete like a jackhammer; sneakers screeched.

"I'm open, I'm open," he shouted.

"I'm open too," I whispered.

Sweat trickled from his brow, and he was starting to develop a nice mocha tan. I imagined that he would look quite handsome sipping merlot on the Amalfi Coast.

"C'mon, Paco, let's go."

There was only so long I could stand there looking like an idiot. Tomorrow would be another day to get ignored.

I saw him at Lamill on Sundays. He ordered an iced Americano and then sped away in his Audi Q5, which was double-parked in a loading zone out front. He smelled of woodsy Old Spice and didn't wear a wedding ring. You bet I checked. I'm not a stalker, I swear. It's just totally weird to keep running into the same person over and over. Clearly, we were on the same schedule; go to Holly Hills Dry Cleaner and that Rite Aid on Western. My friend Heidi said it meant we had messages for each other, but what the hell were they and how was I going to get them if I couldn't make eye contact?

He seemed perfect. I got those jittery butterflies when I reached the court. They skittered across my tummy, but "Richard Gere" still paid me no mind. He reminded me a bit of my ex, Thomas. They had the same kind of goofy smile, gapped tooth top center. But he probably wasn't an insensitive asshole who dumped his girlfriend on a romantic vacation in Cabo. I still couldn't drink a margarita, and the thought of guacamole made me want to vomit. My hands trembled at baskets of tortilla chips. The whole thing turned me into a crumbling heap of dust. But "Richard Gere" wouldn't be like that. I could just tell. He guarded the tall Asian guy in the yellow jersey and dribbled the ball. He wasn't that good. He missed most shots and was shorter than the rest of his team, but he played with a kind of voracious intensity. Cobalt eyes deadlocked on the ginger sphere.

"Hello, hello, over here!" I mouthed.

It had to mean something, didn't it?

A week from Thursday would be the day I would do it. I would have a full week to prepare and gather up my courage. I also needed to figure out the proper outfit to casually walk my pup in and look cute. It couldn't be too slutty or dressy. That would be totally desperate and obvious. I decided on my yellow floral maxi and some gladiator sandals. I curled my long blonde hair into loose, beachy waves just like Gisele Bundchen. Tom Brady wouldn't even know the difference.

The weather had cooled down, but the Santa Ana winds still blew a warm breeze that hugged my cheeks. The palm fronds swayed like lofty green lollipops. He was there as usual, silver mane bobbing up and down. I stopped just beyond the chain link fence.

"You can do this, Sadie; you can do this."

My therapist said it's helpful to repeat positive affirmations to yourself in stressful situations, so I tried. The boys chanted, a whistle blew, and the tall Asian guy in the green jersey and the guy who looked like John Krasinski howled at each other. "Richard Gere" had his back to me, and Paco yapped at the chocolate Labradoodle. He lunged, almost taking me with him.

"Paco, sit!" I yanked him back. He whimpered and gave me that "I'm so cute; don't get mad at me" face, which usually worked, but I had to focus. If I didn't do it now, I never would. All I needed was for him to look at me for thirty seconds. I would smile and say hi and the rest would be history.

"Hey, fuckin' foul!" he shouted.

This game was intense. His face was rosy and bloated, hair drenched. Maybe I should abort and reassess till tomorrow? Paco tugged, and the ball smacked against the backboard with a booming ricochet.

"Foul!" he hollered again, but no one listened. They just kept playing, attempting alley-oops and bank shots. He threw his hands up, turned, and finally looked at me. His eyes were extra bright, and the wind blew his hair into a puffy gray cloud.

"Hi."

He squinted and saluted, shielding the glare. The sun encircled him in an angelic glow.

"Hi!" I shouted and flashed my pearly whites.

"Huh?"

A kerfuffle of dribbling and then the orange globe sailed high and smacked him square in the kisser. Fuck.

– ⚙ –

There was this pretty girl who walked past the courts. She had a yippy dog, like a Yorkie or something, and she stood and watched the game from the chain-link fence. She stayed only for two minutes or so and surveyed the scoreboard. At first, I thought I knew her, but she never said hi or smiled. She was in her own world floating and towing that rat around; a tiny hairball that was not a real dog. There was something off about her, but I couldn't put my finger on it. She kind of reminded me of the little girl from *Poltergeist* but all grown up. She wasn't spooky, but there was an ethereal expression that rested on her lips. When I tried to get a better view, she was already on her way rounding the bend by the rec center, tiny rat prancing in her wake. But like clockwork she was back the next day at 6:15.

We must have lived in the same neighborhood. I saw her at Lamill on Sundays when I grabbed a coffee before driving to Glendale to pick up my kid. She sat at the counter and typed on her laptop while munching on avocado toast. She wore those big gold Beats earphones that swallowed up her tiny head. She was probably at least ten years younger than me.

I had sworn off blondes after my divorce. Dating in Los Angeles blew. If one more chick asked what kind of car I drove or how tall I was, I was going to lose my shit. There was this cult of Kardashian Botoxed bimbos that filled up the apps. Jesus, I should've given up long ago. I already had my shot.

I thought she was following me; it was too coincidental to run into her at Rite Aid and The Oaks. But she never acknowledged me. In fact, she glanced down and rushed away. It was like she was scared. She scampered with quick ballerina steps, messy blonde hair covering her sage eyes. She probably thought, why is this old, creepy guy gawking? Maybe she thought I was following her?

Basketball was my release. It took my mind off work and my ex. I never missed a game, rain or shine. It calmed me down and helped me sleep. After the divorce, I developed a bout of insomnia. I decided to give up. It was a lost cause, and there was no use in making a fool of myself. I didn't want to become that LA cliché. Old guy, pretty young thing. It was nauseating.

Thursday's game was super intense. Chad was such a fucking cheater. The whole team was sick of it, but they were all a bunch of pussies and kept their mouths shut. I wanted to wipe that silly smirk off the cocksucker's face.

"Foul!"

"Fuck you, Andy," Chad said.

It was hot as hell, and it reeked of shit. I wasn't in the mood for the neighboring dog-park stink. I bounced the ball. Chad caught it and dribbled.

"Fucking foul, dickhead."

The prick just continued to grin, dribbled, and then dunked right in front of me. The team played on. I threw up my hands and gave myself a time-out. I chugged some water and let it trickle onto my face like tiny raindrops. I glanced and there she was, standing by the chain link fence. She wore a long yellow dress, and this time she smiled. Her smile was cute and silly with an upward swoop. Her lips moved, but no sound escaped.

"Huh?"

I couldn't hear. The ball was thumping, and the whistle squawked like a five-alarm fire.

"Hi!" she said.

Oh, hi.

Finally.

"Head's up," Chad screamed.

"What?"

And then the auburn torpedo collided with my skull and knocked me to the ground. The rubber scorched the bridge of my nose, and blood oozed down my chin. It was murky, and my cranium sunk into a heavy slumber on the cool court. I could feel the vibrations as my teammates flew from basket to basket. How was I going to explain this to my kid? I sat up and held my head back. The blood was gushing. I could feel it trickle all the way down to my Adam's apple. She was standing at the fence motionless, mouth agape. Crap.

– ✠ –

Sadie wanted to bolt. How was she going to get out of this? He had seen her, and she was to blame for him sprawled out in a bloody heap. She clutched the twisted metal diamonds tighter. The rust branded her palms with copper x's. She should have kept her mouth shut.

"It's you," Andy said.

"What?"

"It's you; you walk your dog by the courts."

"Um, yeah. Are you okay? Do you want me to call 911?"

Sadie took a few paces forward, dragging Paco with her. He barked with his tiny yap, and she tripped on the hem of her sundress. She picked the pup up and scratched him behind his ears. Andy's teammates cackled, were doubled over, and muttered, "Fuckin' foul." Blood caked the front of his beautiful silver mane.

"Fuck off," he shouted, giving them the finger.

It was starting to get dark. The sun was dipping into the magenta horizon, mish mashing the brilliant primary hues. Sadie wasn't usually at the courts this late, and it was cooling down. She should have brought a sweater. The warm breeze snuck up her vertebrae. She was sticky and yet chilly. Goosebumps speckled her forearms, and those butterflies scratched at her belly button like they were trying to march on through. She took a few steps closer and rummaged in her purse to pull out some tissues.

"Here, this might help?" She shrugged.

He took them and shook the water from his bottle above his head and blotted at the cherry ocean.

"Thanks."

"Are you sure I can't call 911? Wow, that looked awful. I'm so sorry. I didn't mean to distract you."

"No, really I'm fine. No worries. It's not your fault."

He studied her through his blurry vision. She kept crossing and uncrossing her legs like she had to use the ladies' room. She glanced from side to side.

"Don't you go to Lamill on Sundays? I think I've seen you at the counter."

"Oh, yeah. That's me. Funny, it's a small world." She tucked a lock of golden hair behind her ear.

The team was watching, lined up like a firing squad hooting and high-fiving.

"They have fantastic coffee," he said.

"I like their avocado toast." She gave a half smile.

He continued to blot, and Sadie fished in her purse for more tissues, but she was all out.

"Okay, well um, yikes. Feel better. You sure I can't call anyone?"

Andy smiled and shook his head. He glanced down and tapped his temples with his forefingers. Sadie started to back away, one toe behind the other like an expert wire walker. He was mesmerized by the concrete, probably about to pass out. The game commenced with more squawks and trash talking. He studied his filthy Jordans and dabbed at his nostrils.

What the hell, you only live once.

"Hey, what's your name?"

But by the time the words soared into the atmosphere, he saw that she was already hurrying away, hauling that rat down Silver Lake Boulevard. He watched as she turned into a tiny sliver of yellowish mist just beyond the chain link fence.

ACKNOWLEDGMENTS

Eternally grateful for your reading, editing, love, and support.
Marilyn Wilker
Ellen Silverstein
Barry Jay
Jill Wilker
Dominique Iturbide
Christine Schwab
Chelsey Emanuel
Amanda Szot
Kristine Newton Sung
Emily Wolfe
Kristen Hansen Brakeman
Asher Hung
Nicole Haner
Suppasak Viboonlarp
Ella Snow
Lynn Hightower
Sally Shore

and

"Mac," who knew I had it in me all along.

MBW

ABOUT THE AUTHOR

Michelle Blair Wilker is a Los Angeles-based writer and producer. Her fiction and essays have appeared in *Across the Margin*, *Whistlingfire*, *Hollywood Dementia*, and *The Huffington Post*. She was a finalist in Glimmer Train's November 2012 contest for new writers and short listed for the Fresher Writing Prize in 2015. In 2017, she attended DISQUIET: Dzanc Books International Literary Program in Lisbon, Portugal, and was featured in The New Short Fiction Series in Los Angeles. Her TV producing credits include *Stand Up to Cancer* and The Grammys.